What the hell had she been thinking?

Zoe paced the length of her living room, arms wrapped around herself. She knew better than to get involved with someone on staff, but when she got near Chris Taylor, she didn't seem to think at all.

A wave of longing shivered through her as she heard his truck drive away.

When he'd kissed her, she felt it down to her toes. Heat flashed through her as she recalled how she lost herself in his arms. He was a passionate and generous lover who held nothing back, expecting no more than her full surrender in return.

The passion they shared was intoxicating, but her vulnerability when she felt herself spinning out of control was scary as hell.

Dear Reader,

Get ready to counter the unpredictable weather outside with a lot of reading *inside*. And at Silhouette Special Edition we're happy to start you off with *Prescription: Love* by Pamela Toth, the next in our MONTANA MAVERICKS: GOLD RUSH GROOMS continuity. When a visiting medical resident—a gorgeous California girl—winds up assigned to Thunder Canyon General Hospital, she thinks of it as a temporary detour—until she meets the town's most eligible doctor! He soon has her thinking about settling down—permanently....

Crystal Green's *A Tycoon in Texas*, the next in THE FORTUNES OF TEXAS: REUNION continuity, features a workaholic businesswoman whose concentration is suddenly shaken by her devastatingly handsome new boss. Reader favorite Marie Ferrarella begins a new miniseries, THE CAMEO—about a necklace with special romantic powers—with *Because a Husband Is Forever*, in which a talk show hostess is coerced into taking on a bodyguard. Only, she had no idea he'd take his job title literally! In *Their Baby Miracle* by Lilian Darcy, a couple who'd called it quits months ago is brought back together by the premature birth of their child. Patricia Kay's *You've Got Game*, next in her miniseries THE HATHAWAYS OF MORGAN CREEK, gives us a couple who are constantly at each other's throats in real life—but their online relationship is another story altogether. And in *Picking Up the Pieces* by Barbara Gale, a world-famous journalist and a former top model risk scandal by following their hearts instead of their heads....

Enjoy them all, and please come back next month for six sensational romances, all from Silhouette Special Edition!

All the best,

Gail Chasan
Senior Editor

Please address questions and book requests to:
Silhouette Reader Service
U.S.: 3010 Walden Ave., P.O. Box 1325, Buffalo, NY 14269
Canadian: P.O. Box 609, Fort Erie, Ont. L2A 5X3

PRESCRIPTION: LOVE

PAMELA TOTH

Silhouette®

SPECIAL EDITION®

Published by Silhouette Books

America's Publisher of Contemporary Romance

Special thanks and acknowledgment are given
to Pamela Toth for her contribution to the
MONTANA MAVERICKS: GOLD RUSH GROOMS series.

This book is dedicated with appreciation to the staff
of Evergreen Hospital in Kirkland, WA, and to
healthcare workers everywhere for taking such good care
of the rest of us when we need you the most.

 SILHOUETTE BOOKS

ISBN 0-373-24669-2

PRESCRIPTION: LOVE

Visit Silhouette Books at www.eHarlequin.com

Printed in U.S.A.

PAMELA TOTH,

a *USA TODAY* bestselling author, was born in Wisconsin, but grew up in Seattle where she attended the University of Washington and majored in art. Now living on the Puget Sound area's east side, she has two daughters, Erika and Melody, and two Siamese cats.

Recently she took a lead from one of her romances and married her high school sweetheart, Frank. They live in a town house within walking distance of a bookstore and an ice-cream shop, two of life's necessities, with a fabulous view of Mount Rainier. When she's not writing, she enjoys traveling with her husband, reading, playing FreeCell on the computer, doing counted cross-stitch and researching new story ideas. She's been an active member of Romance Writers of America since 1982.

Her books have won several awards and they claim regular spots on the Waldenbooks bestselling romance list. She loves hearing from readers and can be reached at P.O. Box 5845, Bellevue, WA 98006.

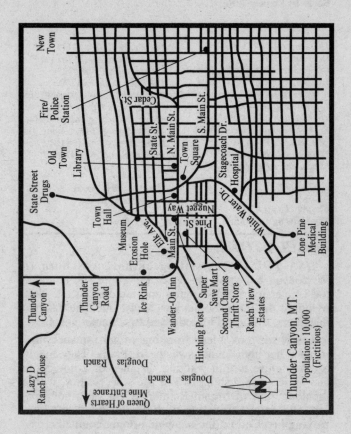

Thunder Canyon, MT.
Population: 10,000
(Fictitious)

Chapter One

When Chris Taylor parted the striped curtains that separated the emergency-room cubicles, he immediately
noticed a pale, frightened-looking young woman lying
on the exam table in a flowered hospital gown. Her tightly
clenched fist was pressed against her mouth, the knuckles a pale contrast to the thin gold band on her finger.
Standing beside her was a tall, bone-thin fellow wearing
an equally anxious expression on his unshaven face.

Carrie, one of the E.R. nurses, had already drawn
blood and started a saline IV.

"This is Dr. Taylor," she told the couple, with a quick
smile at Chris. "Sally Martin, age twenty-two, fifteen
weeks into her first pregnancy, with mild cramps—"

"They won't stop," the man interrupted, twisting a red baseball cap in his big, rough-looking hands. "She took a home pregnancy test a few weeks ago, but she hasn't been to see a doctor yet." He glanced at his wife. "Not a regular doctor."

Understanding what he meant, Chris didn't take offense, nor did he react to Carrie's eye roll from behind the man's shoulder.

The couple didn't look familiar, but Chris wasn't surprised. When he had first come back to Thunder Canyon after completing his residency in Chicago, the small Montana town hadn't changed much, even though its historical setting always drew tourists. A couple of months ago, though, a new vein had been accidentally discovered at the abandoned mine. As news spread about the find, a wave of newcomers, burning with gold fever, had begun pouring in to the area.

From the worn condition of the husband's plaid work jacket and the dirt on his heavy boots, he was probably either a prospector or some type of laborer who had no health insurance. To Chris, who was thirty-two, they both looked young enough to be in high school.

"You did the right thing coming in." He glanced at Carrie, who reeled off Sally's stats and vital signs. Chris wasn't surprised to hear that her pressure was low.

"CBC, type and cross match," he said as a tech poked her head through the curtains. "Sharon, call someone down from Labor and Delivery to consult." A pregnancy of less than twenty weeks would be treated right in the E.R. by one of the OB/GYN residents.

"Yes, Doctor." She left quickly with the vials of blood.

"Are you bringing in a specialist?" The young patient spoke for the first time, her high voice laced with panic. "Am I in labor? Oh, God. It's way too soon!" she cried, clinging to her husband's hand.

"Easy, easy," Chris said calmly. "Try to relax. It's just routine, but we'll know more after we examine you."

Sally bit her lip as tears shimmered in her dark eyes. "I got scared when the cramps started, so I tried to call my mom back in Idaho, but she wasn't home from her job."

Her husband had turned so pale that Chris hoped he wasn't about to pass out. It wouldn't be the first time a prospective father had kissed the tile floor, but it would be a lot more helpful if he stayed strong and supportive.

"When I got off work, Sally had been spotting for a while, so I brought her straight in," he explained, giving his wife an apologetic look. "We only have one car. I carry a cell phone, but the battery went dead."

The tech stuck her head back through the opening in the curtains. "Dr. Hart is on her way down," she reported.

Chris ignored his unprofessional leap of anticipation at the sound of her name. "Why don't you show Mr.

Martin where he can wait until we're done," he suggested. Conducting a pelvic exam was usually less awkward without a husband looking on.

The expression on the man's long face reflected his indecision. "Honey?"

Her lip quivered as she looked up at him. "You go," she said. "I'll be okay." With obvious reluctance, she unpeeled her fingers from their death grip on his hand.

"We'll come for you as soon as we know something," Chris promised as Sharon herded the husband from the cubicle.

Almost immediately, Zoe Hart appeared in his place. Although the stunning brunette had been working at the hospital for several weeks, the jolt of reaction Chris felt each time he saw her always took him by surprise. He did his best to ignore it, since mooning over one of the residents, even one who didn't report directly to him, was a complication that his life didn't need.

"Thanks for brightening up the E.R.," he said with a grin he didn't try to hide, as he got to his feet. "Sally, this is Dr. Hart. She's come all the way from sunny California just to help us out."

The resident's expression revealed nothing, but Sally looked relieved to see another woman.

"Dr. Taylor." As Zoe acknowledged his introduction before giving the patient a perfunctory glance, her voice was as smooth as blended whiskey. "What's the situation?"

"And this is Sally Martin," Chris continued. Sometimes new doctors needed a subtle reminder that they treated people, not just cases and body parts.

Even pressed together into a straight line of obvious annoyance as they were now, Zoe's lips were as sensual and plump as pink satin pillows. He had overheard one of the male residents refer to her as an "ice queen," but more than once Chris had glimpsed a spark of temperament—quickly hidden—in her gorgeous blue eyes. Was there passion beneath her cool facade? One of these days, he was going to find out for himself. But right now, the patient deserved his complete attention.

"I'll check back," he said reluctantly. An OB/GYN resident didn't need his help with a simple exam.

Zoe washed up at the sink and donned her gloves, her cheeks burning from the implied criticism she'd heard in the other doctor's tone. He was the head of the E.R., so she had to be careful.

Just because she didn't ooze folksy charm from every pore like some people didn't mean that she didn't care deeply about her patients, she thought with a spurt of resentment. The ability to focus totally on the condition being presented, rather than allowing herself to become sidetracked by trivial banter, helped her to be a more capable physician.

The sight of Dr. Taylor's shaggy, dark blond hair and rumpled scrubs always made her feel as though she had just stepped onto the set of a soap opera back in L.A., not a genuine—and surprisingly modern—medical center in the wilds of Montana. His chiseled features and brawny build could have been a major distraction if Zoe were susceptible to that kind of rugged hunkiness. But his apparent small-town mentality and lack of vision set her teeth on edge.

According to the overworked and ever-humming hospital grapevine, Christopher Taylor had grown up in this backwater town and he planned to die here. That kind of lazy shortsightedness was a waste of his talents that she was unable to fathom.

While the nurse prepared everything for the exam, she filled Zoe in on the patient's symptoms. There was nothing unusual about the case.

"Nice to meet you, Sally," Zoe said briskly as soon as Carrie was done speaking. "Go ahead and put your feet into the stirrups and scoot all the way down for me, okay? I'll be checking the opening to your cervix to determine whether it's dilated."

The poor girl looked scared to death, her eyes wide and her lips bloodless. "What if it is?" she asked in a small voice as she complied awkwardly with Zoe's instructions, doing her best to keep her gown from sliding up as she moved down.

Zoe felt a tug of compassion that she immediately pushed aside in order to prevent herself from being distracted by emotion. "Then we'll have to do a D&C."

Ignoring Sally's gasp, she proceeded with the exam. When she was finished, she peeled off her gloves and dropped them into the trash can. The husband was brought back to the cubicle and Dr. Taylor reappeared as though he'd been signaled.

"The cervix is still closed, so there's no reason to admit you today," Zoe explained to the patient. "However, bed rest is essential. If the cramping and spotting doesn't stop, it's important that you get medical attention right away."

"I'll make sure she takes it real easy," promised the husband as he stroked his wife's arm.

She remained silent, her eyes still wet from the tears that had started to roll silently down her cheeks at the mention of a possible D&C.

"Good," Zoe replied briskly. "We'll just have to wait and see whether or not you're able to maintain the pregnancy." As she paused for breath, a soft moan escaped Sally Martin's bloodless lips, followed by a flood of fresh tears.

Zoe hesitated. "I'm sorry," she added, feeling inadequate for the first time since she had entered the cubicle. "There's nothing else we can do."

As the husband leaned down to awkwardly pat his wife's shoulder, Zoe glanced expectantly at the head of the E.R. For once his smile was absent, making her wonder if she had missed something. This was a textbook case, she reassured herself, nothing complicated, and she had followed recommended procedure to the letter.

Dr. Taylor gave her a nod of dismissal. "Thank you, Doctor."

With a tiny shrug and a last glance at the prone woman, Zoe excused herself. As she walked away, she heard the other doctor's deep voice as he made a remark about Boise, Idaho—another faux-western town that Zoe had no desire to visit unless it was hosting a medical convention.

Hands tucked into the pockets of her white coat, she blew out a breath as she dodged a scurrying lab tech who was pushing a cart. From the E.R. waiting room, Zoe could hear a child crying. A man shouted and a doctor attempted to calm him. Other voices rose and fell, some loud and others soothing. The phone at the triage station rang repeatedly and somewhere a door slammed. The wail of a siren was cut off abruptly as an ambulance approached the building. From behind a nearby curtain, a doctor snapped out instructions while the surgeon on duty was paged over the intercom.

After Zoe stopped at the vending machine for a chocolate bar, she headed for the elevators and the comparably tranquil environment of her regular department with a feeling of relief. She was a resident in Obstetrics and Gynecology on the second-floor maternity wing. Since her recent arrival at Thunder Canyon General, she had been called down to the E.R. for consultations on several occasions, but she didn't enjoy the often chaotic atmosphere.

"Hey, hey, Doc Hart," exclaimed one of the brash male interns when she passed him. "You been slumming?"

"Looks like," she replied without slowing her stride. Making friends with every horny male staff member who considered himself a player didn't interest her. She couldn't wait to get away before someone summoned her to help out with a new crisis. The E.R. was often understaffed, but her skills were better suited elsewhere.

You never knew what you'd be assisting with next down here—a car accident, burns or some other grisly injury, an unwashed miner with an infected toenail or a patient who puked on your shoes, as a little boy had done all over Zoe's new white Nikes just last week. Despite her best cleanup efforts, the laces were still stained.

Absently she watched for Dr. Taylor as she pushed the up button. Let him keep his quaint western town, his cowboy boots and his laid-back, rural Montana lifestyle, she grumbled silently. She was surprised that he didn't fill in the neckline of his scrubs with a fancy bolo tie—complete with a stone the color and size of a robin's egg.

Even though a unique opportunity had lured Zoe to this hospital, she could hardly wait to complete her residency in Thunder Canyon—which she privately thought of as Lightning Gulch, the hicksville hellhole—so she could return home. She'd only been in Montana for a few weeks, but she was already more than ready to brush the hay from her designer jeans and race back to Southern California with its sunshine, its energy and its gourmet restaurants. She even missed the trendy boutiques and their wealthy, shallow patrons.

If she wasn't careful, she'd turn into Paris Hilton before she realized what was happening.

Despite Zoe's aversion to unnecessary gore, vomit and other body secretions, she was passionate about the practice of medicine, especially women's health issues. The delivery of a healthy baby still made her throat go tight. Her mission, besides completing her residency before she went stir-crazy, was to learn as much as she could from the director of her department.

As the elevator doors finally slid open, spilling out its passengers, Dr. Taylor strolled up beside her.

"Dr. Hart, I'd like to speak with you if you have a moment before you leave us," he said before she could escape. "This way, please." Without waiting for her reply, he led the way in to one of the larger treatment rooms.

Zoe maintained a confident expression, standing as tall as she possibly could while he closed the door. Even if he hadn't been wearing the western boots that looked so ridiculous with his scrubs, he would still tower above her middling height.

Her mind raced as he studied her silently: Refusing to fall into the trap of blurting out something stupid in order to break the uncomfortable silence, she thrust out her chin and waited him out.

"You're a talented doctor," he said abruptly.

She nearly sagged with relief before managing to

catch herself. Apparently his reason for the detour had merely been to pay her a compliment.

"Thank you," she replied.

"You could be better," he added, catching her by surprise.

"Was there a problem with the way I handled this case?" she demanded, bracing her hands on her hips.

Zoe's mother, a successful real-estate salesperson, had warned her that men in authority were sometimes intimidated by confident women. Zoe would rather stand her ground than be run over.

Without his habitual smile, Dr. Taylor didn't look like the type to be easily intimidated by anyone. "Not in the way you're thinking," he said, looking regretful. "The problem, as I see it, is with you, Doctor. I'm afraid you're not showing me something that I consider to be extremely important."

He didn't have a reputation for sarcasm or shouting, not even when someone screwed up or wasn't prepared, so the bluntness of his statement now stunned her as would an open-handed blow to her face.

"W-what do you mean?" she stammered, before she regained her composure.

"I'll bet everything has come pretty easily to you all your life," he mused.

She wanted to laugh at the absurdity of his comment or, at the very least, tell him that he didn't know what he was talking about. However, a lowly resident didn't speak to a supervisor in that manner if the resident wanted a decent evaluation, so she bit her tongue.

"I've read your file," he continued. "You're extremely bright, capable, attractive and obviously ambitious."

"An adequate doctor?" she asked.

The corner of his mouth hitched up. At least he didn't appear offended. "More than adequate."

"Thank you, Dr. Taylor." She realized that he had just complimented her appearance as well as her brain. Perhaps he really just wanted to hit on her. Fraternization between hospital staff members—and not only the single ones—wasn't uncommon in a place where people worked long hours dealing with life-and-death issues on a daily basis. For a supervisor to show a personal interest in someone on a lower rung of the pecking order wouldn't break any rules.

"That young girl you just treated is afraid she might lose her baby."

Like a dash of cold water, his grim words snapped Zoe back to reality. "If you had bothered to look into Mrs. Martin's face before you got down to business," he continued, "I'm sure you would have seen that she needed a little Karo with the medicine."

He hadn't been present during the actual exam, so the nurse must have said something to him immediately afterwards.

"A little what?" Zoe asked, genuinely puzzled.

"Karo Syrup," he explained. "It sweetens things up."

Was Dr. Taylor one of those men who felt that a woman needed to be protected from anything as harsh as the truth, even when it concerned her own body?

"Are you saying that I shouldn't have been straight with Mrs. Martin?" Zoe demanded. "That I should have coddled her like an invalid or a child who needed to be spared from life's harsh realities?"

His blue eyes narrowed, screened by lashes several shades darker than his hair. "Of course not. She's a grown woman and I'm not suggesting that anyone has the right to withhold the truth. But neither does she deserve to be bludgeoned with the possibilities."

"You know she could still lose that baby," Zoe argued. "She and her husband need to be prepared."

He speared the fingers of one hand through his hair, leaving it in tufts that caught the overhead light. "I'm trying to remind you, Doctor, that our responsibility here is to treat the entire patient, not just an anatomy or a symptom. That girl was ready to shatter. Anxiety isn't going to help her situation. Neither is guilt over what she may or may not think she did to bring this on. That's all I'm saying. You could have taken another moment to explain that sometimes miscarriages just happen."

Zoe knew he had a valid point, but she couldn't bring herself to concede. "I'll be so glad when screening is available to measure the protein levels in early pregnancies and identify high risk," she offered instead. "Someday we'll be able to do a lot more than merely recommending bed rest."

Stuck here in the Gulch, he'd probably never heard of the research study she'd read about last week in *The Lancet,* a well-known medical journal, but she couldn't resist the urge to show off.

"Don't get ahead of yourself, Doctor," he drawled, folding his arms. They were deeply tanned and covered with a sprinkling of fine gold hairs.

"A link between miscarriage and low levels of MIC-1 certainly appears possible," he continued. "However, we're still a long way from using either it or its synthetic analogues in preventative treatments, despite what our colleagues in Australia may have discovered." He glanced at an orderly pushing an empty wheelchair past the window. "Let's hope their findings eventually pan out."

"Yes, let's hope," she murmured, impressed despite herself. Obviously the man didn't spend all his spare time on horseback. "Is that all, Doctor? I should get back upstairs. I've got patients."

A muscle flexed in his lean cheek before he inclined his head and made a sweeping gesture toward the door. "Don't let me keep you, Dr. Hart."

As Chris watched the young resident march away with her head held high and the tails of her lab coat flapping, he allowed himself one gusty sigh of frustration before turning back to the triage center. He knew from reading her file that she had finished med school at Berkeley near the top of her class, but he believed brains and talent to be only part of the equation that made a good doctor. Without heart and empathy for the people she treated, she would never be more than a highly trained technician—better suited to a research lab than the treatment of human beings. If he was to influence her in any real way while she was here, he'd have to find a path around her protective wall to the real Zoe Hart.

And he'd have to do so without losing his objectivity, which would be no easy feat considering the powerful pull he felt whenever he got within sight of her.

Glancing at the round wall clock above the check-in counter, he was relieved to see that his shift was nearly over. Dismissing the pretty resident from his mind, he went to find the doctor who was scheduled to relieve him.

A little while later, Chris came out of the locker room wearing civvies and a heavy sheepskin-lined jacket as protection against the unpredictable March weather.

"You have a nice evening, Dr. Taylor," said a voice from somewhere above Chris's head as he dodged the ladder erected in the middle of the hallway.

"Hey, Willie," he replied when he saw one of the longtime maintenance crew climbing down the rungs. "How's your wife's diabetes doing? You making sure she eats right?"

A grin creased Willie's leathery face as he stepped off the ladder. He'd been a bull rider until a hip injury had sidelined him a decade ago. "She's doing good, Doc." Willie hitched up his belt with the big silver championship buckle. "Thanks for asking."

"I'm working with a new pony," Chris said, referring to the gelding he'd begun training to calf rope.

A woman walked by them, trailing the scent of expensive perfume like a feather boa. She gave Chris an admiring glance over her shoulder that he returned absently.

"A Quarter Horse?" Willie asked, his faded brown eyes lighting up with interest.

"Black as a licorice whip. Come on over and see him when you get the chance," Chris suggested.

"I might do that." Willie's pager signaled him, so he folded up the ladder. "Sorry, Doc. Gotta go."

Chris headed out the door to the parking lot before something new could happen to reel him back in to work. Ever since word had gotten out about the strike at the Queen of Hearts mine, the E.R. was too often filled to capacity with the careless, clueless or just plain unlucky prospectors.

As much as he loved being a doctor, he was happy to leave work behind him for another day. One of the advantages of living in a small Montana town was that the commute between the hospital and the farmhouse where he'd grown up with his parents and his three younger sisters took only a few minutes.

The sound of Chris's pickup truck coming down the long driveway alerted Ringo. The mixed-breed Husky raced down the porch steps with his tail wagging madly. Someone had dumped him on the road out front two years ago with a bullet lodged in his shoulder, but there was no lingering evidence of the injury when he ran alongside the truck.

Someday Chris hoped to add a pretty wife and several brilliant children to his impromptu welcoming committee—all waiting eagerly to smother him with hugs and kisses. But until he met the right woman, one who could love the land and the lifestyle as much as he did, he felt no great rush to settle down. For tonight at least, attending to chores and hungry livestock would give him time to figure out a way to crack Zoe Hart's hard shell.

"Hey, buddy," he called out to Ringo after he'd rolled down the window of his truck. "How was your day?"

"I'm homesick," groaned Aretha, a resident from the surgical floor, between bites of her roast-beef sandwich. "I miss my boyfriend."

Silently Zoe poked at her chef's salad as she let the conversation flow around her. No matter which shift they worked, this round blue table was where the residents usually gathered whenever they came to the cafeteria.

"Don't you live in Butte?" asked a redhead named Marty who had recently rotated out of the E.R. into Pediatrics.

"Yeah, she does. Aretha gets to go home every weekend," said a thin guy whose name Zoe had forgotten. He stopped drumming his fingers on the table long enough to push his glasses back up the bridge of his nose. "Boo-hoo," he added sarcastically.

Most of the residents and interns shared units in an old apartment building near the hospital, unlike Zoe. Thanks to her mother's generosity, she rented a small place by herself in a nicer complex. She valued her privacy, but living alone meant that she only knew the others from working with them. Sometimes she felt like an outsider.

"I heard that you had a private tête-à-tête with Taylor down in the E.R. yesterday."

It took Zoe a moment to realize that Barb Hiller was speaking to her. Perhaps because Barb was also a Montana native, like Aretha, she seemed to consider herself the self-appointed leader of the group.

"Oh?" Zoe injected her tone with disinterest as she arched her brows. "Where did you hear that?"

Barb's smile didn't reach her green eyes. "Around. You can't keep secrets in this place." She shrugged her plump shoulders. "Did he chew you out or what?"

"Doc Taylor chewing out an underling?" echoed Marty before Zoe could reply. "Get real. As long as you know your stuff, the man's a teddy bear."

Barb leaned forward, her gaze never wavering from Zoe's face. "Well, maybe Hart doesn't know her stuff."

Although Zoe hadn't yet had the dubious honor of working with Barb, it appeared that the woman had some kind of grudge. Maybe she resented Californians. But her opinion didn't matter to Zoe, who wasn't here to make friends.

"I manage." Without bothering to defend herself further, Zoe began cutting her tomato into smaller pieces.

After a moment of uncomfortable silence, Aretha asked if anyone knew of a good place in town to get her hair cut. Zoe tuned out the discussion that followed. Eventually Aretha got to her feet and picked up her tray.

"Later, you guys," she called over her shoulder as she headed for the bussing station.

Zoe continued gazing around the room as she sipped her lukewarm tea. The area was lucky to have a modern facility as Thunder Canyon General. She had heard that the money to build it had been donated by someone who had lost a family member because the hospital in Butte was too far away.

The interior of the cafeteria was too stark for her taste, but it was clean and convenient. Its white floors were dotted with blue tables and lighter blue chairs. Booths ran along the wall and tall windows faced a courtyard. At this time of year, the outside eating area was empty except for a few benches and a silent fountain.

Today the sky overhead was the same shade of pale gray as the Navy ships she'd seen docked in San Diego. When the snow melted and the temperature warmed up later this spring, the courtyard would be a great place to eat. The tables would probably be filled with people sharing meals. Perhaps there would be flowers blooming brightly among the evergreens, while water cascaded down the face of the fountain.

Even though the view through the windows looked bleak today, it was vastly more attractive than the amateurish mural that someone had painted on one wall of the cafeteria. The trees and mountains had been depicted with clumsy brushstrokes, resembling a children's art project gone awry.

Deciding to forgo the whole-wheat roll that had come with her salad, Zoe was about to slide back her chair when Dr. Taylor approached the table.

"How are you all doing?" she asked, smiling at everyone.

Zoe froze, irrationally afraid for one heart-stopping moment that he intended on making another pointed comment about her lack of empathy with patients. Immediately she realized that she was being paranoid as well as unrealistic. Even though she hadn't agreed with his comments yesterday, at least he'd taken the trouble to deliver them in private, unlike some doctors she'd worked with.

Everyone at the table, including Zoe, responded to his greeting. As usual, he was dressed in light green scrubs with his stethoscope sticking out of the breast pocket and scuffed cowboy boots on his feet. His blue eyes were a startling contrast to his deeply tanned face, and his hair looked in need of a good stylist.

"Would you like to join us?" Barb batted her eyes

invitingly as she pulled back an empty chair next to hers.

He shook his head with apparent regret. "Thanks, but I just wanted to invite all of you who don't have late shifts tomorrow to come out to my place after work for spaghetti with some of the other E.R. residents."

He handed out sheets of paper. "Here's a map, but it's not hard to find. We'll make it five-ish. Casual dress, of course, and bring your appetites. Not to brag, but I'm a pretty decent cook."

"Wow, sounds great," said Vadivu, a soft-spoken resident from India, as she studied the map.

"Free food." The nameless guy's comment drew a laugh. "Can someone with wheels give me a ride?"

"We'll figure it out," said someone else.

"How nice of you, Dr. Taylor," cooed Barb, sending him another big smile. "I'll certainly be there."

Dr. Taylor looked around the table, his gaze touching on Zoe's. "You're included, Dr. Hart."

"But I'm not in E.R.," she protested. "I wouldn't want to intrude."

"Horsefeathers," he replied. "I'll expect to see you there, okay?"

Caught off guard, she had no choice but to accept with an attempt at graciousness. "Of course. Thank you."

For an instant, his grin seemed to widen before his attention shifted. "Barb? Marty? Peter?"

"Absolutely," he replied, touching his hand to his glasses.

Silently Zoe repeated Peter's name, needing to distract herself from the idea of going to the E.R. director's house for dinner. If he hadn't put her on the spot, she would have come up with a plausible excuse.

Her instinct told her to stay as far away from Dr. Christopher Taylor as possible. But now she was committed. If she wasn't careful, she'd develop a crush on him—as Barb seemed to have already done.

Chapter Two

As Chris watched the rowdy group seated around his mother's big dining room table wolfing down green salad, garlic bread and spaghetti, he tried to figure out a way to draw Zoe into the conversation. So far, she had been more of an observer than a participant as they discussed everything from the latest music CD to the dramatic increase of patients coming to the E.R.

If Zoe was upset over his comments to her the other day, she would have to get over it. Everything he had told her was true; she was smart, but she needed to warm up and connect with her patients.

"I think noncriticals should go to a walk-in clinic so they don't clog the E.R.," Barb said loudly, as Chris slipped Ringo a bite of garlic bread. The dog sat beside his chair on the braided oval rug. Its rich colors complemented the wood floor that he'd stripped and refinished, as well as the deep red walls he had painted the winter before. The last time his parents had visited, his mother had said she had always wanted to do away with the flowered wallpaper in this room.

Marty, the redheaded intern from Spokane, took a gulp from his wineglass.

"The only clinic in town isn't set up for that," he argued. Everyone else had nearly finished eating, but Marty was still plowing through a second helping of spaghetti topped with a healthy layer of grated Parmesan cheese.

"Then we should build a walk-in clinic," snapped Barb, tossing her napkin onto her empty plate. She had an opinion on everything from the shift schedule to the nursing staff, and she wasn't afraid to share it.

Tired of hearing her voice, Chris got to his feet and pulled out his wallet. "Well, I've got a twenty," he said as he gave her an exaggerated wink. "How about you?"

Barb looked genuinely puzzled. "I don't understand."

"So when you said *we*, you didn't actually mean it?" asked Vadivu.

Barb flushed. "I was speaking facetiously."

"In the meantime, real people with real problems are overtaxing the E.R., as well as the rest of the hospital," Zoe pointed out, speaking for the first time from her place at the end of the table facing Chris.

She wore a soft blue sweater that hugged her curves like cashmere—not that he was any expert when it came to expensive clothes, since he lived in scrubs and jeans. The golden brown hair that she normally wore pinned up at work had been left loose tonight. Like melted caramel swirling over vanilla ice cream, the shimmering strands framed the creamy oval of her face.

"These people and their children need help now, not later," she added, leaning forward so that her tiny gold hoop earrings caught the light from the chandelier overhead. "How can the hospital turn them away?"

Chris caught her gaze, sending her a smile of approval as he replaced his wallet and sat back down. "Zoe's right. Until people have other options, the E.R. has no choice but to treat them."

Marty helped himself to the last two olives from a crystal bowl that had belonged to Chris's grandmother. "What's with the gold strike?" Marty asked, waving his hands. "Surprise! Hey, if I had a mine, I'd sure as heck know whether or not the thing was tapped out. It wouldn't take some kid falling down the shaft during a blizzard, then popping back up with a nugget clutched in his hot little hand to clue me in."

"He didn't pop up," Barb interrupted. "Dr. Taylor's sister rescued him. She nearly got trapped when it caved in."

The reminder sent ice sliding down Chris's spine.

"I hate to say that Marty's got a point, though," said Peter. "I wondered the same thing."

"Nor could Erik's hand be described as 'hot' by the time they found him," Barb added. "The poor kid was nearly frozen."

"Ha-ha," Marty drawled. "I was speaking in the abstract."

"That's where your mind usually is," Peter replied, poking Marty's arm.

"Behave, children," Barb told them.

"Who owns the mine?" Vadivu asked Chris.

"A man named Amos Douglas won the Queen of Hearts in a card game back in the 1880s," he replied. "The land still belongs to his descendants."

"Douglas?" echoed Marty. "Any connection to the Douglas who's developing the new ski resort?"

Chris nodded. "Caleb Douglas is Amos's grandson. The Douglas family probably owns more land than anyone else in this area." He didn't bother to add that Caleb strutted around town as though he owned Thunder Canyon, too. Chris was surprised he hadn't run for mayor. Caleb must be in his fifties, so there was still time.

"Ah. Has Caleb got any unmarried daughters?" Marty asked, mouth full. "I could use some help with my student loans."

Everyone laughed at his comment. Even Zoe smiled.

"Caleb Douglas has two sons, Riley and Justin." Barb set her napkin next to her empty plate. "Justin's the illegitimate one who married that woman at the Heritage Festival right before the blizzard."

"Oh, you're referring to Katie Fenton, the librarian," Vadivu said. "She's a very nice lady. I just wish the library wasn't so small." She sighed. "Seattle has a wonderful library system, even though the new downtown building looks like a partially squashed aluminum box."

"Have you been to that music museum in Seattle, the one that looks like a crushed guitar?" asked Marty.

Vadivu shook her head. "You mean Experience Music? That's not really my thing."

"I'd love to eat dinner at the Space Needle sometime," Barb said. "What a rush to be that high."

For a few moments, the conversation veered away from the Douglas family tree to unusual places they'd all been to or wanted to visit, and then on to people they missed back home. Once again, Chris noticed that Zoe remained silent, contributing nothing.

"So old Caleb doesn't have any daughters?" Marty asked with a dramatic sigh after he had finished eating.

"Well, none that we actually know of," Barb drawled.

Marty laughed at her comment, but Vadivu looked uncomfortable as she scooted back her chair. "I'll start clearing off the table."

Before Chris could say anything, Zoe also got to her feet. "I'll help."

Her offer surprised him. Maybe just because she came from a fancy part of L.A., drove a new car—when most of the interns and residents were too burdened with student loans to afford wheels—and didn't live in staff housing didn't mean she was spoiled.

"None of this explains why no one knew there was gold in the mine." Marty leaned back in his chair and handed his plate to Vadivu, who accepted it wordlessly.

Annoyed by the younger man's attitude, Chris didn't bother to reply. He didn't tolerate discrimination of any kind in the E.R., so Marty had better watch his step and pull his own weight or Chris would fillet him like a mountain trout.

"Who made you king?" Barb demanded, glaring at the redhead. "Get off your butt and help with the KP."

Rather than appearing resentful or embarrassed, Marty got to his feet. "Same goes, princess," he told Barb with an upward jab of his thumb. He looked at Chris. "Great meal, Doc."

A chorus of agreement accompanied the general shifting of chairs.

"I'm glad you all could make it." Chris picked up the carved-wood salad bowl his folks had sent him from Arizona. "Let's load the dishwasher and then go out and burn off some calories," he suggested. Outside the darkening bay window, the afternoon's snow had stopped and the wind appeared to have died down.

Zoe reappeared in the doorway from the kitchen. "I should probably leave," she said. "Thank you for including me."

His spirits plunged with disappointment.

"No, you can't go yet," Barb exclaimed. "No one

else wants to leave, and you can't expect the rest of us to squeeze into my old beater."

If Zoe was bothered by Barb's bluntness, she didn't let it show. Instead, she appeared hesitant as she nibbled her full lower lip.

Ignoring his instant hormonal reaction, Chris gave Zoe his most engaging grin. "Come on, Dr. Hart. You've got time for a snowball fight before you leave."

He could almost see her withdrawal, as though his choice of address had reminded her that he could pull rank if he chose. Damn, he hadn't meant to imply that he was *ordering* her to stay.

Instead of answering him, she turned around, hands empty, and went back into the kitchen.

A snowball fight? How childish could they get?

For an instant, Zoe had been pleasantly surprised that Barb wanted her to stay, but then the other resident had made it crystal clear to everyone that she was interested in Zoe's taxi service, not her company.

Whether the rest of them liked her or not didn't matter. As frustrated as a cat in a cage, she crossed to the kitchen window, arms folded, and stood with her back to the room and the comments that flowed back and forth.

Refusing Dr. Taylor's dinner invitation wouldn't have been prudent, so she had come. Now that she had put in the obligatory appearance, there was no reason for her to hang around for a romp in the snow.

Even in a group, the man made her uncomfortable, as did this quaint country setting, with its barn and pastures—and animals. She was out of her element—not just here in Lightning Gulch, as she called it privately, but in the wide-open spaces of Montana. If it hadn't been for the lecture she had attended back at Berkeley, given by Dr. Olivia Chester, Zoe would be completing her residency at some huge medical complex in California where she shared her mother's condo.

Longing for temperate weather, Zoe frowned at the fresh snow blanketing the ground outside the window. It was supposed to be springtime, not the middle of winter!

"Zoe?" A hand touched her shoulder.

Stiffening in reaction, she turned to gaze up into Dr. Taylor's ocean-blue eyes.

"Yes?" She tried to back away, but the chill from the window glass seeped right through her sweater, making her shiver.

Immediately he let his hand drop and took a step back, as though he sensed her discomfiture. "Are you all right?" he asked quietly. "Do you really need to leave?"

Barb glanced at them curiously as she walked by with some dirty glasses. Her ears were probably straining to hear what was being said.

Zoe lifted her chin and curved her mouth into a social smile that would have made her mother proud. "I'm fine, thank you. I wouldn't want to break up the party, so I'll wait for the others." She had no idea where the decision had come from, but she was stuck with it now.

"Are you sure? I can drive people back to town later if you must go," he offered. He seemed to be studying her, which made her wonder if he was assessing her for a report.

Standoffish? Doesn't play well with others? She could imagine the words written on some secret evaluation that weighed her and found her lacking. *Doesn't fit in?* Why did she always have to assume that she would come up short in the eyes of her peers? Surely not everyone in her life saw her inadequacies as clearly as did her parents.

"That's not necessary," she replied. "But thank you for offering." Maybe he *wanted* her to go.

For an instant, he leaned closer, his gaze darkening. "That's a lot of thank yous," he murmured. "Be careful, Zoe, or you'll owe me."

Shock left her speechless, feet rooted to the floor, as he straightened and turned away. What had he meant by *that?*

"Come on, people," he called, clapping his hands as though he were herding children out to recess. "There are spare gloves and hats in the mudroom in case anyone needs them. Boots, too. So no excuses."

He probably shouldn't have added that last comment about owing him, Chris thought as he zipped his parka and pulled a stocking cap down over his ears.

The last thing he wanted was to give Zoe the wrong impression or make her feel inappropriately pressured. Teasing someone like her was too darned tempting, especially when he saw the way her big blue eyes had widened with alarm. Or maybe it was Zoe who was tempting. He would have to be careful.

Meanwhile, he had snowballs to make.

In just a few moments, Chris and his residents were all running around like a band of noisy children. In the artificial glow cast by the overhead yard light, a barrage of fat white missiles, whoops of triumph and shrieks of dismay filled the air as they scrambled to hit each other. Even Ringo got into the mix, barking excitedly as he darted among the noisy combatants.

The worst of the battle was over quickly. The snow had been trampled underfoot, leaving churned peaks that resembled mounds of whipped cream. Marty lay sprawled on his back on the ground, still chuckling helplessly. Barb's face was flushed and her dark jacket was splotched with white, evidence that she'd been a popular target. Their breaths formed pale clouds, and Ringo sat on his haunches with his tongue hanging out.

Relatively unscathed, Chris scooped up more snow and compacted it as he turned in a circle, searching for Zoe. He had been too busy dodging snowballs to spot her during the skirmish. After he'd practically insisted that she stay, the least he could do was make sure she didn't escape completely unscathed.

She was standing alone on the sidelines, her purple

jacket and dark pants hard to notice in the shadow of
the utility shed. Just as he saw her, a cold, wet snowball hit him squarely in the back of his neck and slid
down inside his collar.

With a yelp of surprise, he hunched up his shoulders
and turned around to glare at his assailant with as much
menace as he could manage. Several feet away, Vadivu
was nearly doubled over with laughter. Her black eyes
sparkled with horrified glee, her gloved hand covering
her mouth, while the pom-pom on top of her red-and-
yellow-striped hat bobbed like a big fat dandelion.

"I'm sorry!" she gasped between giggles. "I was
aiming for Barb, I swear."

"Hey, why me?" Barb demanded hotly, brushing the
snow from her jacket.

"Let's wash Vu's face!" Marty cried as he scrambled
to his feet. "I'll hold her."

Vadivu's laughter turned to puzzlement. "What do
you mean about washing my face? It's already clean,
and water would freeze my poor skin out here."

"He's talking about rubbing snow on your face, not
water," Zoe explained, stepping closer. "It's a barbaric
custom perpetuated by little boys who refuse to grow
up."

"Oh, really?" Chris drawled, as Marty lunged play-
fully at the Indian girl. She ducked, shrieking loudly,
and scooped up handfuls of loose snow that she tossed
at him before she spun away. Marty gave chase, restart-
ing the battle as he pelted her, too.

Ignoring the shrieks, Zoe stood her ground as she watched Chris warily. The harsh utility light drained the color from her face, leaving a pearly glow to her cheeks. Her knit cap, with its topknot, matched the black fur trim on her jacket. The outfit made her look as though she belonged on some trendy ski slope with the rich and famous, not his trampled-up stable yard. He would guess that her clothes set her further apart from the other residents, who wore a hodgepodge of styles that could have come from the local thrift store, Second Chances.

Chris allowed himself one long look at Zoe before bending down for more snow. As he did, a snowball flew past his ear and struck her square in the face.

Zoe didn't see the white blur coming in time to duck. She barely managed to shut her eyes before it hit. For one stunned moment, she couldn't breathe, couldn't see a thing, because of the sudden burst of cold. Vaguely she heard a shout of triumph. As she stumbled backward blindly, firm hands steadied her.

"Easy," Dr. Taylor said softly. "Don't fall over or they'll be on you like a pack of wild dogs."

Breathing through her mouth, Zoe wiped the snow from her face. Thank goodness for waterproof mascara. That and tinted gloss, to protect her lips from getting chapped, were all she had bothered with after work. Her hair, freed from its clip after work, was probably hanging in wet strings around her chapped and blotchy cheeks.

Charming. All she needed was for her red nose to start running. Or glowing, like Rudolph's.

"Hold still." Dr. Taylor had removed one glove. His hand was warm against her skin as he leaned down to carefully brush away the snow that clung to her face and hair.

Zoe had never been this close to him before. When he caught her staring, he went still and their gazes held for a timeless moment while the sounds around them seemed to recede. His grip tightened on her shoulder, his eyes darkening with awareness as she forgot to breathe.

"Hey, Doc," someone called, shattering the moment of intimacy. "Can we see your horses?"

He waved his hand without turning his head. "Welcome to Montana, Zoe," he said softly.

She frowned, her cheeks blooming with heat despite the cold air. "I beg your pardon? In case you haven't noticed, I've been here for several weeks."

"Oh, I've noticed," he drawled. "But you haven't truly arrived until you've been pasted in a snowball fight."

"Oh." Her voice sounded small to her ears. Without thinking, she let her gaze drop to his mouth. Its shape was mesmerizing.

What would it feel like to kiss him?

The unbidden thought shocked her right down to her slightly numb toes. Her knees nearly buckled. Horrified, she jerked her attention back to his eyes. His expression had sharpened, as though he knew exactly what she'd been thinking. The notion flustered her even more.

No matter how she felt inside, she never allowed her feelings to show. So this temporary lapse had to be from the high elevation. It was the chilled air that made her head spin.

"N-now I really do need to leave, if the guys who came with me are ready," she stammered, heart thudding. "I've g-got some reading to finish before my shift in the morning." She was babbling, but she couldn't seem to stem the flow of words. "I'm assisting Dr. Chester with surgery at seven, so I have to read up on the procedure."

His expression changed, losing its intensity as he pulled on his glove. "Olivia's a treasure. You can learn a lot from her."

"She's the reason I came to this godforsaken wilderness," Zoe blurted thoughtlessly.

He went as still as a statue. "What do you mean?"

Had he thought she actually liked being stuck out here? She hadn't meant to offend him, but she had forgotten for a moment that he was a native son. He had told them tonight that he'd grown up right in this house. Thanks to the hospital grapevine, no one had any real secrets, and everyone had known that already.

She also knew they called her the "ice queen," but she didn't care.

He was frowning, so she couldn't very well ignore

his question asking what she'd meant by her tactless remark.

"When I was at Berkeley, I attended one of Dr. Chester's lectures on women's health," she explained. "She described her work in rural and depressed areas, and the clinics that she's helped to open and run. I was impressed. She's made a real difference."

When he remained silent, Zoe shrugged self-consciously, reluctant to elaborate on her own career goals and reveal too much of herself. "It's a field that interests me," she tacked on lamely. Why did she let him continue to shake her normally unshakable poise?

The dog's barking distracted them both. Dr. Taylor glanced over his shoulder and Zoe noticed part of the group heading toward the stable. Vadivu and the other girl who had ridden with Zoe were standing near the back porch, deep in conversation. She hoped they didn't mind leaving now, because she was in desperate need of some time alone to decompress.

"Looks like I'd better start the tour of the petting zoo," Dr. Taylor quipped. "Sure you won't stay a little longer? I can promise to show you some real live horses."

She knew from his tone that he was teasing, but she figured she had monopolized his attention for long enough, even though she hadn't asked for it.

"I've seen horses before," she replied drily. "But thanks again for dinner. It was very nice."

"No problem. If you like to ride, you're welcome to come out anytime." His smile was open and friendly.

Maybe the personal interest she'd thought she had noticed had been merely a product of her own arrogance, and he was only trying to be nice.

Not every man is after you, her mother had commented once after Zoe had complained about a neighbor's beady stare.

"I don't ride western." She hadn't meant to sound so stuck-up.

"A pity." His grin widened. "But I reckon you could learn, little lady. You look fairly bright."

She nearly laughed at his terrible accent. "I, um, left my purse in the house." She waved at the other two girls. "Ready?" she called.

Vadivu nodded. "Anytime." Like Zoe, she spent a lot of time cracking the books in the staff housing she shared with two other girls. Once, she had commented that she came from a big, noisy family, so living in bedlam wasn't a bother. Zoe used to envy girls who came from big families.

"Go ahead and get your things from the house while I wipe the snow off your car," Dr. Taylor offered, heading toward the driveway.

There was no denying it—in addition to being as attractive as an actor on a TV soap, he seemed genuinely nice. Zoe usually went for sophisticated, uncomplicated and shallow, so why did her radar go nuts whenever the head of the E.R. came in range?

She didn't think she'd like the obvious answer, so she ignored it.

A few minutes later, she and her two passengers were on their way. Vadivu sat in the back, so the blonde in the passenger seat—whose name Zoe had forgotten—sat turned half-around so the two of them could discuss one of the lab techs from work.

"He looks like that guy from *Scrubs,* only cuter," said the blonde.

Zoe hardly ever watched television. With nothing to contribute, she tuned out their chatter. The road back to town was curving and she didn't have a lot of experience driving in snow, so she gripped the wheel tightly and watched for icy patches on the pavement ahead.

The houses they passed were scattered and most of them were surrounded by barns and other outbuildings, just like Dr. Taylor's place.

His house had been a surprise, since she'd expected something modern and showy, or rustic yet pricey like a couple of the log homes she'd driven past in the daytime. Instead, he lived in a boxy, old-fashioned farmhouse with deep porches and antique furniture.

The interior was attractive, if you liked that kind of decorating style. The wooden floors were refinished to a warm glow. The walls were freshly painted and covered with wainscoting and wood trim refinished in sparkling white. The kitchen and the powder room had been modernized, too, with granite counters and pewter fixtures. Anyone could see that he—or someone—had spent a lot of time fixing it up.

As her car approached the lights of town, such as

they were, and the other girls finally fell silent, Zoe smothered a yawn. Social situations were always a little stressful, especially those with co-workers. Perhaps she found them so because her parents always seemed to combine business with pleasure. Growing up, Zoe had been expected to act in a certain way because— whatever the occasion—it seemed that there were always clients or other people underfoot. As far as she could remember, the only family milestone that hadn't taken place in front of witnesses had been the final breakup of her parents' marriage.

"Zoe?"

From Vadivu's tone, it was clear that she had been trying to get Zoe's attention from the back seat while the other girl—Megan, Zoe remembered suddenly— looked at her expectantly in the glow from the dash lights.

"I'm sorry?" Zoe glanced in the rearview mirror, but it was too dark to see Vadivu's face.

"What were you and Dr. Taylor talking about for so long?" the Indian girl asked.

The directness of her question caught Zoe off guard. She didn't know any of the other residents very well, since she didn't live with them, but she and Vadivu had sat together in the cafeteria on several occasions. The girl seemed nice enough.

"Um, we were discussing a patient," Zoe replied.

"What a bummer." Megan sounded disappointed. "You looked way too intent to be talking shop."

"Dr. Taylor is so handsome," Vadivu added with a dramatic sigh. "And you are so beautiful."

Her comment surprised Zoe, who wasn't used to getting compliments from other women.

"Thank you," she said, steering carefully through a bend in the road. "I wish that I looked exotic, like you." She had seen the attention Vadivu attracted at the hospital. In addition to her black eyes and long, straight hair, she had clear golden skin and full red lips.

"Which case were you discussing with him?" Megan asked persistently. "Something gory?" Her features were plain and her hair was frizzy, so perhaps compliments about appearance made her feel uncomfortable.

Zoe thought quickly as she flexed her fingers against the steering wheel. With sudden inspiration, she described to them the young woman who had been so worried about a possible miscarriage.

With Ringo at his side, Chris stood gazing after the taillights on Zoe's car until they had disappeared from sight. Then man and beast walked back up the driveway to the stable yard.

For the most part, the residents were a bright group and he enjoyed working with them. There was something, though, about Dr. Hart that especially intrigued him—both in and out of the hospital.

"Did the party poopers leave?" shouted Marty as he appeared around the corner of the utility shed. He'd had several glasses of wine with dinner, Chris had noticed at the time. His face was still flushed. It might well be from the cold, but Chris was glad Marty hadn't driven out tonight, or he would need a designated driver to transport him back to town.

"If you're referring to three of your colleagues, the answer is yes," Chris replied pointedly as he joined the younger man, grinning to soften his comment. "Let's find the others before they turn my horses loose."

Chris was careful not to comment when Marty stumbled over a rut in the snow. It didn't matter if the younger man was hungover in the morning, since he had already mentioned having a day off. Since Marty had great rapport with patients and was fast on his feet in the sometimes hectic E.R., Chris hoped he didn't have a problem with alcohol.

As they walked through the open stable door, Chris felt the familiar sense of harmony descend on him, draining away his fatigue. He truly believed medicine was his calling, but spending time with his horses always served to renew his spirits. That was probably the reason he kept a couple of extra mounts available for anyone from work who might want to come out and ride.

"Phew," Marty quipped, fanning his hand in front of his nose, "smells like a barn in here."

Chris didn't bother to respond. Instead, he went straight to the stall where Denver, his new black gelding, was holding court like a king with his subjects.

Barb extended her hand, palm up, for Denver to

sniff. "What a beautiful animal," she exclaimed, rubbing his nose. "Quarter Horse?"

"That's right," Chris replied proudly, pleased that Denver didn't appear fazed by his visitors. "He comes out of the gate like a loaded spring."

The horse's ears twitched, and then, angling his head, he grabbed for the pom-pom on top of Barb's hat.

With an easy laugh, she ducked away. "No you don't, you big clown."

"Whoa, look at the size of those teeth." Marty hung back, wide-eyed. "Good thing it's not a carnivore."

"For you, he might make an exception," Barb said.

The occupant of the stall next to Denver's, an old palomino named Queen, whacked the wall with her hoof in a bid for attention. After Chris had slipped her a carrot from the nearby bin, he moved down the row to greet the rest of his horses with a word or a touch. He had spent a lot of time out here over the years, mucking out stalls, fixing tack and doing other chores with his dad while they talked about everything from feed mixes to character qualities.

"Do you show some of your stock?" asked one of the other residents, peering into the open tack room. Along with the saddles propped on stands and other gear hanging from hooks on the wall was a display case full of ribbons and trophies.

"I compete in local rodeos when I have the time," Chris admitted. Before he'd grown too tall and sanity had prevailed—much to his mom's relief—he had dreamed of becoming a professional bull rider like Willie.

"What event?" Barb asked, sitting down on a bag of feed. "I used to barrel race back in high school."

Chris wished that Zoe had stuck around. He wondered if she liked animals.

"I'm training Denver to calf rope." He loved the sense of teamwork between rider and mount as they bolted after the calf, of knowing just when to cast the loop and leap from the saddle as the horse braked. Chris would scramble down the taut rope with a pigging string clamped in his teeth, then toss the calf and tie three legs together as quickly as possible, thrusting his hands in the air to stop the clock. Talk about an adrenaline rush!

"Do you raise cattle, too?" Peter asked, nervously pushing his glasses up the bridge of his nose as he did whenever he presented a case.

"Just a few head," Chris replied. "My day job doesn't leave me a lot of time to play rancher." He glanced at his watch. "Speaking of which, I'd better kick you all out so you can go home and get some sleep. Morning comes early."

They filed out of the stable and he closed the door. Back at the house, they gathered up stray possessions, thanked him again for dinner and sorted out who was sitting where in the car. As they trailed back outside under a canopy of stars, they were arguing good-naturedly.

Barb was the last one to alight after patting Ringo's head. This time, Chris didn't stand around in the cold and wait for the departing taillights to disappear into the night as he had when Zoe had left. Hands stuffed into his pockets, he whistled for Ringo and headed back inside to enjoy the blissful silence.

Chapter Three

Zoe's next day off work fell on a Saturday, so she decided to take full advantage of the break. Because of her heavy schedule at the hospital—increased even more since the town's population had begun to swell thanks to the gold fever—she hadn't yet had the chance to explore downtown Thunder Canyon with its kitschy western theme. Except for work, the gas station and a few quick trips to the grocery store, Zoe had hardly gone anywhere.

Briefly she toyed with the idea of calling Vadivu or one of the other residents, but they were probably all either working or sleeping. Having grown up as an only child, Zoe didn't mind doing things by herself.

The sun was shining and the temperature was surprisingly mild. Bypassing the purple parka hanging in her closet, she grabbed her green suede jacket and slipped it on over a cropped, white cotton-knit sweater and tan jeans.

When she stepped outside and slipped on her sunglasses, the air felt downright balmy compared to the chill when she'd left work the night before. An elderly patient had told her that a twenty-degree temperature rise in one week, from snow to shirtsleeves, wasn't unusual in these parts.

Tossing her purse on the passenger seat, Zoe backed her white Honda from its assigned spot and headed downtown. With a popular song on the CD player, she drove past joggers in shorts and kids riding skateboards on her way to the older part of town. The buildings there had been erected during the first mining boom.

She found a parking spot on a side street by a thrift store called Second Chances, where she had overheard one of the nurses say she took her kids' clothes when they got too small. When Zoe walked past the shop, a bearded man and a woman with long hair were looking in the window at a display of tools and furniture. A little girl in a worn pink coat tugged on the woman's arm, but she paid no attention. When Zoe smiled at the child, she ducked her head.

Next door, a tub of rainbow-colored primroses competed for attention with a ceramic pot filled with early crocus and variegated ivy vines. Back home, the flower

beds would already be a riot of color and there would
be hanging baskets everywhere, dripping blooms like
jewels.

She passed an antique shop and a used bookstore,
both busy with customers, and a small teriyaki café
with tables on the sidewalk out front. Loud, choppy
music, laughter and the smell of sautéed garlic spilled
from the open doorway.

Someday when the sky overhead wasn't as blue as
the Pacific Ocean, she might take time to explore the
former schoolhouse that had been turned into a local
museum, or the souvenir shop with its racks of baseball caps and T-shirts. Wouldn't her mother love a black
one with *COWBOY UP!* spelled out in multicolored
sequins across the front?

The image of Patrice Hart wearing a garment without a designer label made Zoe smile.

For today, she was content to wander down Main
Street with its false-fronted buildings and old-fashioned
streetlamps. As she studied the window displays, she
dodged a woman with three kids and a pair of teenagers
with their arms entwined. Most of the people she passed
appeared to be in pairs or groups, but some—like
Zoe—were alone. A few faces looked vaguely familiar, as though she might have treated them at the hospital. Two people nodded; one smiled, and a man with
bulked-up, tattooed arms did an abrupt U-turn when he
caught Zoe's gaze. Her cool stare wiped away his leer.
Grumbling to himself, he hurried away.

As she was walking, a maintenance worker from the hospital touched the brim of his cowboy hat. "Hello, Dr. Hart," he said politely, stopping in the middle of the wooden sidewalk. "How are you doing this fine day?"

The title still gave her a quiet thrill. "I'm enjoying the sunshine," Zoe replied, returning his smile. "How about you, Willie?"

He held up a paper bag. "Been to the hobby shop to get some glue. You be sure to stop by The Hitching Post for a bite if you haven't been yet," he added, pointing back down the street as he backed away. "Tell Martha I sent you and she'll treat you real good."

As soon as Zoe waved goodbye, a delicious aroma wafted past her nose. Despite the bagel and coffee she'd eaten earlier, she was suddenly hungry. Perhaps she would check out Willie's suggestion and eat something before she went back to her apartment.

The Hitching Post was across the street from a historic-looking old hotel called the Wander-On-Inn. Going through the door into the bar and grill was like being transported back through time. In the dim light from the wagon-wheel chandeliers, The Hitching Post appeared to be one big open room. Half was crowded with tables and chairs, most of them full. A long bar made of dark wood curved along the other wall. Above it hung a painting of a woman, nude except for a wisp of sheer material that was strategically placed.

A gray-haired woman was seated at the register by the door. "Are you meeting someone?" she asked.

"No, I'm alone," Zoe admitted, feeling slightly self-conscious. She hadn't expected the place to be so busy. Perhaps she should have stopped at the little teriyaki café on her way back to her car instead, but it was too late now. She wasn't about to retreat.

The bun on top of the hostess's head quivered as she waved a menu to get the waitress's attention. "Table for one!"

Several diners turned to stare. Head high, Zoe followed the waitress, who was obviously pregnant, to a small table near the empty dance floor.

"I'm Juliet," the petite Latina said with a shy smile. "I'll be right back to take your order."

After Zoe decided on a spinach salad and iced tea, she leaned back and glanced around the busy room. Most of the other tables were occupied, as were all of the stools lined up along the bar. She imagined that the place really came alive at night with a band playing live music on the stage and the dance floor packed with people intent on enjoying themselves.

All of them doing something that involved flailing arms and swirling petticoats, she thought with a sly grin.

"Dr. Hart, would you mind if I joined you?"

She jerked up her head to see Dr. Taylor standing over her with his hand clamped on the back of the empty chair. She had been so busy studying the decor that she hadn't been aware of his arrival. So much for feminine radar.

"I'd hate taking up another table when it's so busy, unless you're waiting for someone." Along with his usual dazzling grin, he was wearing a T-shirt with a faded logo under a denim jacket and snug jeans.

She felt cornered, but she couldn't very well say no. "Help yourself," she replied with a smile. "I'm just grabbing a bite between errands."

She had no reason to explain herself or to be concerned about him wondering why she was alone on her day off, but she wanted him to know she was in a hurry so she wouldn't have to stick around and chat.

As soon as he sat down across from her, the waitress appeared with another menu. "Hi, Chris," she said cheerfully as she handed it to him.

"Juliet," he replied, glancing down at her ankles. "How are you, and how have you been feeling?"

Her cheeks turned pink. "Pretty good, all things considered."

Zoe took the opportunity to study his face. His skin was that of a man who spent time outdoors, with tiny creases fanning out from his thickly fringed eyes. His profile was that of a Remington bronze. His bones guaranteed that he would still look great at seventy, no matter how many lines he developed along the way or how silver his hair turned.

If he had any hair left. Right now, it looked obscenely thick and silky—and in need of a good stylist.

"Zoe, have you decided?" he asked, shattering her attempt to picture him without hair.

She blinked, realizing that Juliet was waiting, pencil poised. Quickly Zoe reeled off her order.

"Dressing on the side," she added automatically.

"Cheeseburger, rare, fries and tartar sauce," Dr. Taylor said without opening his menu. "And a root beer, please."

"I'll get that right out," Juliet promised.

"She shouldn't be on her feet so much," he muttered, wearing a concerned frown as he watched her waddle away. "It's too bad she can't afford to take some maternity leave."

"How far along is she?" Zoe asked.

He shrugged. "I'm not sure. You're the expert, so you tell me."

She snorted. Her mother would have cringed at her inelegant gesture. "Hardly that, and women vary too much to sight-read them by how much they show, especially ones as small as Juliet."

They watched the waitress leave their order with the cook before hurrying over to clear the empty dishes from a nearby table.

"Is there a husband or a boyfriend in the picture?" Zoe asked curiously.

"I have no idea," he said. "She doesn't talk much about herself."

They fell silent as their beverages were served, and Zoe scrambled to think of another topic to keep the conversation going. An older man sitting with his family waved at Dr. Taylor, who smiled and nodded. Having been raised here, he must know everyone in town.

"How did your surgery with Olivia Chester go?" he asked Zoe. "What was the procedure?"

Zoe was surprised that he would remember something she had mentioned during the snowball fight a few days before. "It was a C-section because of the mother's preeclampsia."

When a pregnant patient developed high blood pressure, causing a decrease in the blood supply to the placenta, a Cesarean was required. Dr. Chester had allowed Zoe to do most of the procedure herself.

"I'm happy to report that the surgery went well and they're both doing fine," she added, trying to suppress her elation.

"You can learn a lot from Olivia," Dr. Taylor replied after he'd taken a pull on his soda. "She's a talented OB."

A shapely redhead wearing a cropped tank top and low-cut jeans stopped at their table on her way past. She put her hand with its maroon nails on his arm and gave him a fifty-megawatt smile.

"Christopher! How wonderful to see you."

Zoe recognized her from the hospital accounting office and the way she strutted through the cafeteria trolling for dates.

"Hello, Renee," he replied, glancing at Zoe. "You must know Dr. Hart."

"Of course," Renee murmured, barely glancing at Zoe before turning the full wattage of her green eyes back on Dr. Taylor.

"You should call me," she said, flexing her fingers as though she was testing his muscles before she released her grip on his shoulder. Another woman was waiting for her by the register up front.

"You have a great day," he replied. "Enjoy the sunshine."

When Renee left, Juliet set their plates in front of them, saving Zoe from having to comment. "Can I bring you anything else?" the waitress asked. There were dark smudges beneath her eyes, as though she wasn't getting enough sleep, and her delicate face looked too thin despite her body's bulk.

There were worse things than being stuck in Montana for a few months, Zoe thought, as both she and Dr. Taylor shook their heads. She dribbled dressing on her spinach salad while Dr. Taylor dug into his meal.

"You're not a vegetarian, are you?" He picked up half of his oversize burger, dripping juice on his plate. "I don't want to gross you out or anything."

Purposefully she speared a piece of the bacon from her salad with her fork and held it up. "Not everyone from California is a vegetarian, but thanks for asking."

The muscles of his jaw flexed as he chewed. "Thanks for sharing your table," he said when he'd swallowed.

"No problem, Dr. Taylor." Compared to Renee's seductive purr, her own voice sounded prissy and uptight. She had been around more intimidating and successful men than this one without losing her poise, so what was her problem now?

"Why don't you call me Chris when we aren't at work." He flashed a lethal smile that she felt right down to her toes. "Then I could call you Zoe."

She nodded as she jammed a forkful of salad into her mouth. The sooner she finished, the quicker she could get out of here, away from the jumpy way she felt whenever she was around him.

Between bites, he plied her with questions that she managed to answer without revealing too much.

"This place must have a story to tell." She wanted to switch his attention away from her, so she studied their surroundings as he ate a French fry. "Was it always a bar and grill?"

As he blotted his mouth with a napkin, his expression suggested that he knew very well what she was attempting to do. "It started out as a saloon, one of several in this part of town," he said. "The bar's original and so is that painting. It's hard to miss, isn't it?"

Zoe turned to study the figure of the well-endowed blonde. "Is that the woman sitting by the front door?"

His loud bark of laughter caused several people to look their way. "Martha Tasker?" he exclaimed, then immediately lowered his voice as he leaned across the table. "I don't think our Martha is quite old enough, despite her perky gray bun. There's a rumor that the original owner posed for the portrait, but I don't know if it was ever confirmed. The locals call her 'the shady lady.'"

"I'll bet this town rocked on Saturday nights back in the day, during the original gold rush," Zoe mused.

"If you're interested in local history, you should look at the old photos hanging all over the walls here." He bit into another fry. "Have you been to the museum yet? It's housed in the original schoolhouse."

She shook her head. "Today's the first chance I've had to come downtown. Until now, I've only gone to the strip mall at the other end of town." She wanted to keep him talking so she could sit and watch him. What made one person ordinary and another so attractive? "When was gold discovered the first time?" she asked, taking a sip of her iced tea.

"The boom lasted for three decades back in the late eighteen hundreds. I imagine it was just like in the movies, full of saloons, brothels, prospectors and hookers. Then the gold ran out and a lot of people moved on, looking for the next big strike, I suppose. Luckily many of the buildings down here have been preserved or restored."

"And now there's another strike and the town is full of modern-day prospectors," she said. "What do they hope to gain? Isn't the mine on private property?"

"That doesn't stop them," he replied. "They probably tell themselves that there's got to be more gold than just what's down in the Queen of Hearts."

"Oh, that's right," Zoe remarked, interested despite herself. "I forgot about mines having names, just like ships. Is the family that owns it descended from the original prospector to find gold there?"

"It's funny that you should ask," he said expansively,

"because I just happen to know that Amos Douglas won the mine in a card game and then he passed it down." He lowered his voice and glanced around. "Between you and me, they'd better be able to prove their claim because you can bet that someone will check it out now that gold has been found again."

"They must have a deed to the land," Zoe said.

He shrugged. "I'm sure they do. Caleb Douglas is no dummy when it comes to business. He's right in the middle of developing his big fancy ski resort, so I'll bet he could use a little extra gold to help finance it."

"You say that with a sneer in your tone, as though you aren't a skier," Zoe remarked. He certainly appeared to have an athletic build, so he was no couch potato.

He shrugged. "I've done some cross-country, but going down hills so you can take a lift back up seems kind of pointless to me. How about you?"

"I took all kinds of lessons when I was a kid," she admitted. "But I didn't start skiing until college."

He arched a brow. "Ski team?"

She almost giggled, which shocked her. "Ski *trip*," she corrected. "Winter break and a boyfriend I wanted to impress."

His smile seemed to flicker. "Serious?"

She hadn't given Howie a thought for years. "I thought it was until I sprained my ankle and he deserted me for the slopes and a bunny named April."

Amusement danced in his eyes. "Playboy?" he asked.

This chuckle she didn't bother to suppress. "Snow bunny."

"Can I get you anything else?" asked Juliet, stopping at their table.

Zoe blinked, distracted. She had forgotten all about getting away from here ASAP. "No, thanks," she told the waitress. "I have to go."

"Would you like this on one check?" Juliet asked.

"Yes, thanks," Chris said.

"No, that's not necessary!" Zoe protested. She always paid her own way.

Juliet glanced back and forth, obviously confused.

Chris's smile widened, etching grooves into his lean cheeks. "It's only lunch," he told Zoe. "Let me treat you."

She could feel her face go hot. Before she could answer, Juliet laid down two tickets. "When you sort it out, you can pay up front. Thanks for coming in."

Chris figured that he knew when to advance, as he had when he'd first seen Zoe sitting alone, and when to retreat, as he did now when she shook her head.

"I can't let you do that," she said.

He looked forward to the opportunity to push her buttons, but not today. Rather than argue, he slid the tab for the salad and iced tea across the table with his finger.

"Something tells me that offering to arm wrestle you for this wouldn't be a good idea," he teased, watching her reaction.

What was it about the particular arrangement of her features, each beautiful in itself, that combined to form a face that stole his breath each time he saw her? More than what he could see, it was what he sensed that she kept hidden that intrigued him the most.

Zoe picked up the slip of paper and pushed back her chair. "You're a smart man for a cowboy," she said as she stood up.

The full wattage of her smile, aimed straight at Chris, nearly stopped him like a deer caught in the high beams. He stumbled to his feet, as flustered as a kid still in middle school.

By the time he recovered, she was halfway across the room. Rather than attempting to close the gap, he stood back and enjoyed the view of her retreating figure in her snug tan jeans. Only when he caught Juliet staring at him with a puzzled expression did he pull out his wallet and amble toward the door.

It wasn't until the next day when he saw Willie in the hospital corridor that Chris began to wonder if he'd been maneuvered like a steer in a rodeo ring.

"Hey, Doc," the maintenance worker called out, wiping his hands on a rag he then stuffed into his back pocket. "Did you go to The Hitching Post for lunch yesterday like I suggested?"

Chris studied him through narrowed eyes, suspicions gathering like thunderheads forming above the mountains. Willie had made a big point of recommending the bar and grill when they'd run into each other down on Main Street. Chris remembered asking him whether Martha was paying Willie to send her customers.

"Since when do you care where I ate?" Chris demanded when Willie caught up with him.

The bunch of keys that Willie always wore made a jingling sound when he walked. The grin creasing his weathered face seemed to falter and his gaze slid away. "I don't give a rat's arse where you eat," he blustered defensively.

Chris slowed him down with a hand on his wiry shoulder, which tensed beneath Chris's grip. "Anything I should know?" Chris asked.

Willie stood his ground, his expression defiant. "Like what? Can't a guy recommend a restaurant without getting the third degree?"

The idea that Willie might have done something to orchestrate Chris's meeting with Zoe was beyond ridiculous. He realized that there was no way to pursue the subject without looking like an idiot.

With a rueful grin, he patted the older man's back before letting him go.

"Forget it, okay?" Chris jammed his hands into the pockets of his scrubs. "I've got to go."

Was it Chris's imagination or did Willie look relieved? "Yeah," he said. "No big deal." With a nod, Willie hurried away, keys jingling.

Chris shrugged off his suspicions, preferring to recall the unexpected pleasure of the impromptu lunch. If he saw Zoe, maybe he would ask if she'd enjoyed it, too. Meanwhile, he had just enough time before his meeting to drop in on Olivia Chester up in Labor and Delivery, just to say hello.

"Any problems with your patients?" Dr. Chester asked Zoe, who was seated at a desk in L&D, adding chart notes on the women she'd seen so far today.

Zoe returned the director's smile. Dr. Chester was in her fifties, but she was one of those women whose appearance grew more striking with age. Her streaked gray hair was cut short and straight above brown eyes brimming with intelligence. Her olive skin emphasized her lovely cheekbones and the graceful line of her jaw. She was reed thin and always wore khaki slacks with her lab coat. Her only ornamentation, a possible concession to her Navajo heritage, was a pair of small silver earrings set with turquoise stones. On her hand was a matching ring.

"The results of the pelvic ultrasound came back on Candace Burns," Zoe reported. "It confirms an ectopic pregnancy."

"Your suspicion was right." Dr. Chester folded her arms across her chest. "How far along is she?"

"Fifteen weeks," Zoe replied after she'd glanced at the chart. "Her symptoms are too severe for expectant management."

"Is she bleeding?"

Zoe nodded. "And she's experiencing some cramping."

"What options are you considering?" the director asked.

"I want to put her on medication first in order to avoid surgery and the possible risk of damage to her fallopian tubes," Zoe replied, relieved when Dr. Chester nodded in assent.

"You'll have to watch the hormone levels closely," she cautioned.

Zoe nodded. "If they don't drop or if her bleeding doesn't stop, surgery will be her only option."

Dr. Chester's expression softened. "Have you told her?"

"Not yet. I had two deliveries this morning." Zoe glanced over at the dark-haired nurse seated nearby, who had assisted her both times. As usual, Beth Ann wore a smock with a teddy-bear print.

"Make sure your patient understands that this doesn't rule out her chance of having normal pregnancies in the future," the director reminded Zoe before walking away. "Talk to her soon," she said over her shoulder.

Zoe pushed back her chair and got to her feet. "Right away, Doctor."

After the director left, Beth Ann glanced at Zoe. "You'll do fine," the nurse said with an encouraging smile.

Dr. Taylor came up to the counter. Immediately Zoe

wondered what the head of the E.R. would be doing in the maternity wing. "Is your boss around?" he asked.

"She was here a minute ago," Beth Ann replied before Zoe could open her mouth. "I'll go see where she went."

He turned his smile on Zoe. "Nice to see you again. You look very…" He hesitated for a moment as his gaze swept over her. "Very professional," he concluded.

She really had to get used to running into him without overreacting, she thought as she resisted patting her hair clip to make sure it was still in place. He was probably too used to having women fall at his feet.

"Nice to see you, too," she managed to say without stammering. "If you'll excuse me, I've got a patient."

"Is she in labor?" he asked.

"No." Briefly Zoe described the situation with the ectopic pregnancy. "Her test results just came back, so I need to go over them with her."

"That's rough," he replied with a shake of his head.

"But it could certainly be worse," Zoe pointed out. At least they had caught the condition early enough to avoid serious complications. "Her tube could have ruptured, making future pregnancies less likely."

His eyebrows lifted. "I hope that's not quite how you're going to describe the situation when you see her."

Zoe swallowed her annoyance. "Of course not, but that's where she should focus."

"And she will do that in good time, Doctor." He

spoke slowly, deliberately, as his gaze held hers. "But first keep in mind that she will need to mourn this baby, this precious little life she's never going to know. Especially if it's her first."

Zoe hadn't thought of the situation in quite that way. "You're right," she conceded after a moment. "Thank you for the reminder, Dr. Taylor."

"You're welcome. And I enjoyed our lunch," he said, his smile returning.

"Me, too," she admitted.

"Am I interrupting something?" Dr. Chester asked from the end of the counter. Her expression was inscrutable.

Zoe's face flamed. "No, Doctor. I'm just on my way to deal with the ectopic pregnancy," she said without thinking.

"The patient has a name, Dr. Hart." The director's voice was edged with quiet rebuke.

"Of course. I'm sorry." Furious with herself, Zoe bit back further excuses before they could spill out and make her look defensive as well as incompetent. Her slip of the tongue would only confirm Chris's—Dr. Taylor's—previous impression that she had no heart.

Head held high despite her embarrassment, she went to tell Candace Burns the bad news.

"Something I can do for you?" Dr. Chester asked Chris, arms folded across her chest. The amusement dancing in her dark eyes told him that she had heard his comment to Zoe about lunch and that she knew exactly why he was *really* here on the second floor, despite whatever he said.

"It was my fault that Dr. Hart misspoke," he explained. "She was just telling me about it, so the term was probably right on the tip of her tongue."

"No need to defend her," Olivia replied, reaching across the desk for a folder. "Dr. Hart is a talented physician." She flipped it open and scanned its contents. "And a pretty woman," she added drily.

Chris glanced around to make sure there was no one else within earshot. "I agree on both counts. I haven't observed Zoe getting rattled in the E.R., not even when they brought in that prospector with the metal spike through his forearm, about two centimeters from the radius. The poor man skewered himself when his rope broke."

"I heard about that," she replied. "Wasn't your sister with the rescue team that saved him?"

Chris nodded. "Oh, yeah. Faith gets around."

"How is she doing?" Olivia asked, setting aside the folder and resting her hip against the edge of the desk. "I haven't seen her for a while."

Chris knew that his sister had discussed her fertility concerns with Olivia, so he wasn't breaking any confidences. "She's engaged to Cam Stevenson, the guy whose son she pulled from the erosion hole. The nugget in his fist is what started this stampede," he said with a grin. "Cam's a teacher at the high school and he seems like a good guy."

After all the pain Faith had experienced when her ex walked out on her, Chris was pleased to see her find happiness again.

"That's wonderful news," Dr. Chester agreed. "She's a very brave woman in more ways than one."

"That's true. Little Erik was damned lucky that she and Cam found him when they did." Chris had to grit his teeth against the sudden rush of feelings every time he recalled the incident.

After his sister had rescued the boy, the access hole had collapsed, nearly burying her alive. Somehow Cam, who had gone there with her, had managed to pull her out right before Chris arrived with the ambulance. He could still remember the fear that had ripped through him when he first saw her, badly scraped up and covered with dirt. God!

Chris swallowed hard. "Erik is a terrific kid," he told Olivia. "He and Faith have really bonded, even aside from her relationship with Cam."

Olivia's expression softened, making him wonder if she had ever longed for a family of her own. "Your sister has a big heart as well as a brave spirit."

It was time for Chris to change the subject before they both got weepy. "As we were saying, I believe that Zoe will make an excellent doctor," he concluded.

If Olivia had doubts about his impartiality, she didn't bother to voice them. Instead, she leaned closer, wagging her finger in his face.

"Be careful," she warned gently. "Our smart young

resident has made no secret of the fact that she can't wait to leave here when her residency is done. She's heading back to civilization as she knows it."

Olivia's comment made his stomach lurch, even though Zoe's plans were no surprise. "Then our town will lose a promising doctor." He could hear the defensiveness in his voice. Was his attraction that transparent?

Olivia straightened off the edge of the counter. "Somehow I just can't picture you treating gunshot wounds at some E.R. in downtown L.A., or sucking fat from the thighs of rich matrons in a tony Beverly Hills clinic."

"Whoa," he exclaimed, holding up his hands as he backed away. "Don't pack my bags just yet. My roots are here. I'm not going anywhere."

Chapter Four

When Zoe came back from talking to the patient with the ectopic pregnancy, she was relieved to see that Dr. Taylor had apparently disappeared. Ever since she had run into him at The Hitching Post, she couldn't seem to keep herself from thinking about him despite the fact that they had nothing in common except for medicine. Their lives couldn't be more different.

After a moment's hesitation, Zoe knocked softly on the open door to Dr. Chester's office. Its soft green walls were part of the pastel color palette of the entire maternity wing, which was separated from the rest of the hospital by a double set of doors for security purposes.

"Mrs. Martin wants to wait until her husband can be here with her to discuss her situation," Zoe said when the director looked up from her desk. "He's coming straight from work."

"And you're able to wait around until then?" the director asked.

Zoe knew the question was purely rhetorical. Flexible hours and interrupted nights were part of the job as an OB/GYN. "Of course."

The other woman smiled and sat back in her chair. "You're doing a good job, Doctor." She steepled her fingers beneath her chin. "You should be proud of yourself."

Her comment caught Zoe off guard. For a moment she merely stared. If she had been pressed to name someone she respected, Olivia Chester would head the list.

Zoe swallowed hard. "Thank you."

Dr. Chester nodded. Perhaps she was leading up to something, a complaint from a patient or criticism by another staff member. Zoe suspected that a couple of the nurses didn't care for her style. She lifted her chin, keeping her expression blank. "Is there anything else, Doctor?"

"Dr. Taylor seems pleased with your work in the E.R. as well." Her dark eyes sparkled. "I see a bright future for you."

Voices from behind Zoe caused her to look around. She saw Archie, an elderly hospital volunteer, coming out of a birthing suite at the other end of the hall. He pushed a new mother in a wheelchair. Tucked into the bend of her arm was an infant wrapped in a pink blanket and matching hat. Walking behind them was a man wearing black leather and a huge silly grin. He carried a bunch of pink and white balloons in one big hand and a bouquet of roses in the other.

Watching the little parade come down the corridor, happiness radiating from them like a Palm Springs tan, Zoe felt a pang of appreciation. The baby was a preemie that modern medicine had given a chance to thrive.

"There's a happy little family," the director observed quietly.

Zoe realized that she had come over to stand in the doorway. "I'm sorry," Zoe exclaimed, stiffening. The last thing she wanted was for her boss to think she was easily distracted, unable to focus. Emotional.

"There is one more thing," Dr. Chester said. Her smile deepened the creases bracketing her mouth and eyes. Beauty radiated from her, contradicting the current belief that a woman's complexion must be as smooth as a baby's butt for her to be considered attractive.

Zoe braced herself.

"If you haven't eaten yet, why don't you take your break now," the director suggested with a glance at the wall clock. "Someone can page you when Mr. Martin arrives. I'm giving a presentation in Butte later, so I'll be leaving in a little while." She paused to make a notation on a form in front of her. "Dr. Codwell will be on call if you need him before the shift change."

Zoe hoped that she didn't. He smoked cigars and the odor, which she abhorred, always clung to him.

Dr. Chester went back to her desk, leaning down to open a file drawer, which let Zoe know she had been dismissed. As she headed downstairs to the cafeteria, she replayed Dr. Chester's comments in her head.

You should be proud of yourself.

What Zoe had yet to figure out was how to make her parents proud of her, especially when both of them were far too busy with their own successful lives to notice anything she did.

She was on her way to the cafeteria when Barb, the E.R. resident she didn't especially like, came rushing up and grabbed her arm.

"There's been some kind of mining accident," Barb exclaimed breathlessly. "They just paged me. Can you help? The E.R.'s shorthanded and the casualties are five minutes out."

"How many?" Zoe asked, hurrying behind her.

Barb glanced over her shoulder without slowing down and nearly ran into a crash cart that was being moved from one department to another. "At least one critical and maybe two serious from what I heard."

Resigned, Zoe abandoned her dinner plans. If she was lucky, she might have time to hit the vending machines before she was called back upstairs to see the Martins.

* * *

With a final flourish of his pen, Chris signed the release for Harlan Voss, the last of the three prospectors who had been brought in by ambulance an hour earlier. It was a real struggle for Chris to keep his feeling of disgust from his voice and expression, but he knew from experience that morons like Harlan got even more defensive in the face of criticism.

"I hope you learned a lesson from all this," Chris told him.

Harlan sat in a wheelchair, waiting for his ride. His arm was in a sling and there was a dressing on his forehead to protect the fresh stitches. His eyes were bloodshot—whether from his belated tears of remorse or the booze that he and his buddies had consumed before their ill-fated treasure hunt, Chris neither knew nor cared. In the past few weeks, he had seen too many patients like Harlan and his buddies.

"Getting drunk and then deciding to climb a rock wall could very well have been a lethal combination for one or all of you." Chris lectured him sternly. "In the future, do your partying at one of the saloons here in town and then call a cab. It's a lot less risky."

"Yeah, Doc, I hear you," Harlan mumbled, his gaze sliding away like a lizard scrambling for cover. "Is Brad gonna be okay?"

"He's lucky your cell phone worked out there," Chris replied, "because that's not always the case and the nights can still be brutally cold at this time of year."

The man sitting in front of him blanched and then he swallowed hard. "Yeah, I hear you."

"They're running tests on your friend now, checking his brain activity. The results will take a while," Chris continued.

Brad had lost his footing, taking the other two men down with him and sustaining a serious head injury when he landed at the base of the wall. Chris could still picture the fear carved onto the face of Brad's wife when she'd rushed into the E.R. with their two children in tow.

"What about Drew?" the man persisted. "How's his shoulder?"

"As far as I know, he's still in surgery." Chris felt a trickle of frustration. These injuries had been preventable. Even sober people had no idea what they were facing with the terrain, the climate and the wildlife.

"You're the lucky one," he went on mercilessly. "That gash I stitched up on your forehead is going to leave a real macho-looking scar. Your friends aren't so lucky. At best, they'll both have big hospital bills to pay. At worst…" He let his shrug say the rest.

"Aw, God!" Harlan buried his face in his hands. "If they come out of this okay, I promise that I'll never take another drink."

Chris had heard it all before. Catching a glimpse of Zoe Hart as she walked by the main desk, he tossed Harlan's paperwork into his lap. "You do that."

"Hey!" Harlan exclaimed as Chris walked away. "What's your problem?"

Chris didn't bother with a reply. Instead he went after Zoe.

"Thanks for helping out down here," he said when he caught up to her. "With Marty and a couple of the RNs out sick, we're really shorthanded."

Zoe returned his smile with a brief twitch of her lips. "No problem."

"So, you off work now?" Chris persisted, feeling a little too much like a high school nerd hanging around the prom queen.

"I wish," she replied, her expression rueful. "The couple I told you about is waiting for me upstairs."

Like every doctor, Chris was well aware of the risks involved when a fertilized egg attached in a patient's fallopian tube rather than the uterus. "I'm sorry," he said sincerely.

She glanced up again, her tiny gold earrings winking in the light. "Me, too. Giving bad news is the worst part of this job."

He hated letting her go, but then inspiration struck. "Have you had a chance to eat?"

Her expression turned wary as she fished a candy bar out of her pocket and held it up. "Three food groups—fat, nuts and sugar."

"I don't think a nutritionist would agree with your assessment," he said, arching his brow.

As she shrugged, he surprised himself—and her, if the look on her face was any indication—by grabbing the candy bar from her unresisting fingers.

"You don't want to settle for this," he scolded. "You'll need something more substantial." He snapped his fingers as though he'd had a sudden brainstorm. "I've got paperwork to do. Why don't you come by when you're done with your appointment and we'll grab a burger at the diner. You can tell me how it went."

She mulled over his offer, clearly undecided.

Before she could answer, he waved the candy like bait. "If you say yes, I'll split this with you for dessert."

Zoe burst out laughing. "But it's mine!" she exclaimed. "You stole it from me."

Before she could attempt to grab it back, he tucked it into the pocket of his shirt and folded his arms across his chest. "Prove it," he said, offering her his most engaging grin.

Eyes narrowed, Zoe shook her finger at him. "When it comes to chocolate, I don't share," she warned.

Pleased to see that he had slipped past her mask of reserve, he patted his pocket as he backed away. "Ah, but I do. Come by my office when you're done."

"Thank you anyway," she said, looking smug as she pulled out another candy bar and displayed it well out of his reach. "I'm afraid you'll have to eat alone."

What a stupid remark she had made earlier. Zoe scolded herself silently as she came back down the stairs forty-five minutes later and headed for the exit. She doubted very much that a man as ruggedly appealing as Dr. Taylor—Chris—ever ate alone except by choice.

Absently she reached in her pocket as she crossed the lobby, wishing she hadn't been so quick to refuse his invitation to go out for a burger. She probably should have stopped at the cafeteria, but the idea held no appeal. Since she hadn't been to the grocery store lately, her dinner choices were either the candy bar she had taunted him with or drive-through fast food.

An older couple carrying a bouquet of pink flowers and a big stuffed dog entered through security at the hospital entrance. From their happy expressions, Zoe figured they were probably visiting a new grandchild.

"Good night," called the guard as Zoe reached the door.

Before she could return his sentiment, his gaze continued on past hers and he straightened like a soldier coming to attention.

"Good night to you, too, Dr. Taylor," the guard added.

Stepping into the cold night air, Zoe glanced back to see Chris following her out. He was dressed in a bulky jacket and a black Stetson.

"'Night, Rudy. Take care," he told the guard.

The sight of Chris in the western hat made Zoe understand the fascination cowboys stirred in some women. For an instant the upper half of his face was shadowed by the wide brim, turning him into a masked desperado.

His altered appearance sent a shiver of reaction coursing through Zoe. She blinked, clutching the collar of her coat, and the image disappeared when he moved his head.

"Hungry?" he asked, accompanying her toward the employee lot. "Between us, we've got dessert covered, unless you've already eaten yours."

She wondered whether he had been watching for her. The chance to talk shop with someone who shared a common interest instead of eating alone in her car on the way to her empty apartment was suddenly too appealing to turn down twice in one night.

"I'm starving," she admitted as two staff members she didn't know walked past without looking their way. "If the offer of a burger is still open, I accept with gratitude."

The shadow from his hat failed to hide his grin. Was she making a mistake in not keeping her distance, or was she misinterpreting friendliness for flirtation on his part?

"I'm parked right over there." He pointed to the same red truck she had seen next to his barn. Tonight it sat in one of the reserved spots at the front of the employee lot. "I'd planned on going by the co-op to buy feed, but they're closed now. I'll do it tomorrow. Do you want to ride together?"

"I'll meet you at the diner, okay?" she said. "It's not that far."

Let him think she was too stuck-up for his truck, but she always liked keeping her options open. Driving herself gave her the choice of leaving whenever she wanted rather than depending on someone else for transportation. Besides, this wasn't a date, it was just eating together.

"Sure thing." Even though the parking lot was secure and well lit, he waited while she got into her car before walking to his truck. When they got to the diner, there were two empty parking spots out front, so she pulled into one and he took the other.

At the entrance, he removed his hat and held open the door for her. Even though the diner was crowded, the hostess, a gum-chewing blonde, greeted him by name and showed them to a booth right away.

"Thanks, Stella," Chris said, setting his Stetson on the seat beside him.

"You betcha," she replied with a brief glance at Zoe. "Mindy will be right over for your order."

"Have you eaten here before?" he asked Zoe as he picked up his menu. "Their burgers are the best in town."

"Vadivu and I came here once after working a late shift together," she replied, scanning the list of burgers. She was starved, despite the nerves fluttering in her stomach. Perhaps she would splurge on fries instead of a salad with her sandwich.

The waitress, an older woman with a frizzy gray perm, wrote their order with a pencil from behind her ear. After she left, Chris sat back in his seat and fixed his gaze on Zoe.

"So how did your conference go?" he asked.

With a sigh, she moved the salt shaker to the other side of the napkin holder. "Okay, I guess." She was still affected by the memory of the couple's stricken faces. "I don't know what else I could have said to make them feel better."

His smile was sympathetic. "I know it's hard to tell someone they don't have a viable pregnancy. You just do the best you can."

No wonder he was so popular at the hospital. His bedside manner must be fantastic.

Zoe appreciated the chance to talk to someone who understood. Isolation was the flip side of not having to share her living quarters, but sometimes she thought that having the company of a roommate might be nice, too.

"Mr. and Mrs. Martin were understandably shaken up," she said, recalling the tears the couple had shared, hands tightly linked, as she had explained the situation to them as gently as possible.

A wave of reaction threatened to choke her. Startled, she swallowed hard as she struggled to regain her composure, hoping that Chris didn't notice her momentary lapse. Keeping control was so much easier when she blocked out the patients' emotional reactions.

"Relating to your patients on a human level isn't a bad thing," he said quietly. "As long as it doesn't get in the way of sound professional judgment, the ability to empathize with what they're going through makes us all better doctors."

"You told me before that I lack that ability," she replied a little stiffly, trying not to recall the look of devastation on Mrs. Martin's round face.

Chris appeared startled. "I wouldn't have worded it quite that harshly."

"You probably have no idea *what* you said," she blurted.

Luckily the people around them appeared too engrossed in their own conversations to notice, but Chris surprised her by slapping his palms on the table between them and leaning forward.

"My comment, Dr. Hart, was that you're brilliant as well as gorgeous."

Zoe spoke without thinking just as the waitress brought their orders. "You never said 'gorgeous.'"

What was wrong with her that she kept making comments without thinking first? The man facing her seemed to have a talent for disrupting her brain function like a lead shield blocking an X-ray.

"That was an omission I won't make again," he replied.

"Anything else?" the waitress asked after she'd plunked down the red plastic baskets and fished a bottle of ketchup from the deep pocket of her apron.

"No, thanks." Chris's attention didn't shift away from Zoe's face. "You?"

"No, thanks." The aroma wafting up from Zoe's burger made her light-headed. Perhaps it was merely hunger that scrambled her thinking, not the handsome male seated across from her.

Mindy laid their bills on the table and departed silently as both of them dug into their food. While Zoe nibbled on a few of the crisp hand-cut fries, Chris demolished nearly half of his burger. He took a long drink of the root beer and then he squeezed a pool of ketchup next to his fries.

"Sorry for eating like a ravenous wolf," he said with an unapologetic grin. "I couldn't help myself."

Zoe peeled back the wrapper of her burger. "No problem." Following his lead, she took a large bite.

"Your parents must be proud of you," he said while she chewed blissfully. "Any other doctors in your family?"

Mouth full, she shook her head as a little boy in the booth behind her began to fuss. A gaggle of teenagers walked by, talking loudly and elbowing each other as though they were afraid no one would notice them if they weren't obnoxious. A woman in a fringed vest made a selection from the jukebox, swaying to the old Elvis song that began to play.

"So what do they do?" Chris persisted over the noise.

Between bites, Zoe slid into the kind of social banter that had been drilled into her since babyhood. "My mom sells real estate and dad's in The Business."

"The Business?" Chris echoed, looking puzzled.

For a moment she had forgotten that she wasn't in L.A. "Movies," she said shortly.

She hated talking about the subject because people always expected him to be famous, like Spielberg and Tarantino. "He's a director. Most of his stuff goes straight to video."

To distract Chris from more questions, she asked one of her own. "How about your family? Do they all live around here?"

"Just my sister, Faith," he replied. "She's with County Rescue, out of the firehouse. Maybe you've seen her bringing someone in."

Zoe shook her head, ignoring the child behind her who was kicking the back of her seat. "I saw her picture in the newspaper after she saved that little boy. She's very pretty."

"Don't let her hear you say that," he replied with a grin. "My sister is already a pain in the butt." For a moment, his smile faltered and his gaze dropped to the basket in front of him. "Naw, that's not true," he corrected himself. "I'm proud of her. When she's not pulling people out of collapsed mine shafts, she works at the sporting-goods store. Have you been in there?"

"Me?" Zoe asked with a laugh. "No way."

He tipped his head, studying her. "Not the outdoor type?"

"Not really." Zoe's idea of roughing it was a hotel without room service. "What about the rest of your family? What do they do?"

"My folks moved to Arizona after dad retired and both my other sisters followed the lure of big-city lights."

"Where do they live?" Zoe asked, surprised that she had finished her burger without noticing.

"Missoula."

She burst into laughter, having expected him to say

they lived somewhere like Portland or Seattle. But *Missoula?*

"What?" he demanded, looking puzzled. "What did I say that's so funny?"

How could she possibly explain? "Nothing." She waved her hand in a gesture of dismissal before eating a pickle slice that had fallen out of her sandwich. "I'm sure Missoula is very nice."

His gaze narrowed suspiciously, but he didn't press her further.

"And you've always lived in Thunder Canyon?" she asked.

When he told her that he had gone to medical school in Chicago, their conversation drifted briefly back to their careers while she ate the last of her fries and he drank his soda. When she glanced at her watch, she was stunned to see that an hour had passed since they'd arrived at the diner.

"I didn't realize it was so late," she exclaimed, picking up her bill. "I need to get going."

"Yeah. Me, too." He slid from the booth and got his wallet from his pocket.

She ignored the little flicker of disappointment that he hadn't tried to talk her into staying longer. Maybe the time *hadn't* flown for him.

After he'd put on his hat, he helped her on with her coat. She could feel his breath against the sensitive skin of her neck. For a moment she tried to imagine what a real date with him would be like.

"How was everything?" asked the cashier when they paid for their burgers.

"Very good, thank you," Zoe replied.

"Best burgers in town," Chris added.

Zoe zipped up her coat as he opened the door. After the cozy warmth of the diner, the brisk wind was like a slap in her face.

"The temperature here goes up and down like the stock exchange," she grumbled as they walked to their cars. "It's warm back home."

"I hear that you don't have real seasons in California," he replied. "How can you appreciate summer if you haven't had to get through the winter first?"

"I don't need snow to make me appreciate a little sunshine," Zoe argued.

When they reached her car, he waited with his hands stuffed in his pockets for her to find her keys. "Thanks for keeping me company," he said quietly.

"Thanks for suggesting it." She unlocked the door and got in while he held it open. "You were right about the food."

Before she could pull it closed he leaned down, and she forgot to breathe.

"I'll see you at work," he said. "Take care."

Before she could recover her ability to speak, he straightened, his expression in shadow.

This dinner had been a mistake, Zoe realized, her heart thudding as he sauntered away. One that she wasn't about to repeat.

Chapter Five

"Anyone home? Hey, Topher, you here?" called out a familiar female voice.

Only one person still called Chris by that particularly annoying childhood derivative of his name. It never failed to set his jaw, which was no doubt the reason she persisted.

He was in the laundry room where the noise from the washing machine's spin cycle had probably drowned out his sister's knock on the door. He pushed the button to start the dryer load of towels and underwear.

"Yo, Faith, I'm in here!" he shouted. "Faith!" Wiping his hands on his jeans, he shut the door behind him and walked into the kitchen.

She stood inside the back door with Ringo, who gazed up at her with naked adoration on his furry face.

"Hey," she said, smiling. "I was beginning to think you'd fallen down the basement steps."

"Hey, yourself," Chris replied, attempting to glare without much success. "I'm training Ringo to attack anyone who calls me that."

The dog ignored Chris.

Smiling sweetly, Faith unzipped her jacket. "Got any coffee?"

"I'll make some." He gave her a quick hug. Even though a certain amount of harassment was part of his duty as a big brother, the two of them had always been close.

Before he dropped his arm, she pressed a kiss to his cheek. "If I'm not interrupting, that would be nice," she said.

Chris busied himself with the coffee. "You're saving me from doing housework," he said over his shoulder, "so bless you for that. Where are Cam and Erik? I thought that since you got engaged, you three have become inseparable."

"They're spending the day doing guy stuff." She got a dog biscuit from a cookie jar shaped like a fireplug and gave it to Ringo, who accepted it carefully and carried it over to the rug by the back door.

Faith pulled a bar stool out from the island and made herself comfortable. "Cam's gone from being overprotective of Erik to being determined to make up for lost time. Last week, Cam signed him up for baseball. Today they drove into Butte to go swimming."

Chris set the sugar bowl on the counter and got out two mugs while the coffee perked. "Weren't you invited to go with them? I thought Erik was nuts about you."

"He is, just like his dad." She rested her elbows on the counter and wrinkled her nose. "I have to work this afternoon, so I thought I'd come out here and bug you first. How's the new horse working out?" She had watched several of Chris's calf-roping competitions in the past.

"Denver's coming along. I'm taking him over to Shorty Carlstrom's spread to run a few calves next week."

"Your life must be a thrill a minute," she drawled. "How do you stand all the excitement?"

"It's a constant struggle," he deadpanned. "Speaking of thrills, have you set a date yet?"

Seeing the way her sudden smile filled her face and lit up her eyes nearly brought tears to his own.

"We're discussing it."

He tipped his head to the side as he studied her. "When you aren't heating up the sheets?" He considered the blush that stained her cheeks to be fair payback for calling him by the hated nickname "Topher."

"Sounds like you could use a little sheet-heating of your own, big brother," she remarked. "Don't tell me you've already run through all the single nurses at TCG."

"I'm saving myself for someone special." If she knew he was attracted to anyone, she'd never let him forget it.

"She's out there," Faith said softly. "Don't give up."

"Why is it that people in love want everyone else to be paired up as well?" he demanded without expecting a reply. Their mother bugged him all the time to settle down with someone and give her grandbabies.

"We want everyone to be as happy as we are," she explained. "Ever since he pulled me from that erosion hole, my life has changed so much...." She glanced away, but not before he glimpsed a sheen of moisture in her eyes.

He knew that commenting on her momentary weakness would make her uncomfortable, so he pretended not to notice as he filled two mugs and slid one across to her.

"You deserve to be happy, Sis." He had to clear his throat to get rid of the lump. "You know I'm glad for you," he added.

When they'd been kids, he had always been able to provoke her temper and then play the innocent when their parents questioned them. Despite the normal teenage power struggles, he and Faith had always shared a stronger bond than he felt with his two younger sisters. Since Faith's bitter split from her ex, she and Chris had grown even closer.

For a moment, they were both silent as they blew on their steaming coffee.

"You going to the pub for the St. Pat's Day celebration?" he asked.

She nodded, tucking a strand of blond hair, lighter than his own, behind her ear. "I think Erik has something after school so we'll be along later."

"Half the hospital will be there after work as usual." He sipped his coffee. "Have you heard from anyone in Missoula?" he asked reluctantly.

"Hope called a few days ago." Faith rolled her eyes. "As usual, she and Jill were bickering about something or other, but I didn't pay a lot of attention," Faith admitted. Despite their frequent squabbles, the younger Taylor siblings shared an apartment.

Chris reminded himself that it was only natural for them to be closer to their elder sister than to him, but it still stung a little. The only time either of them called him was to ask for help, usually financial.

"They resent me." He didn't realize that he'd spoken aloud until he noticed Faith's startled expression.

"No, that's not true," she protested, reaching over to pat his arm. "They just want to feel independent."

It was his turn to roll his eyes.

"Give them time to grow up," she urged. "You aren't responsible for the choices they make."

He fiddled with the handle of his mug. "You're right. I guess old habits just die hard."

Their parents had always made it clear that they expected him, as the eldest and the only boy, to watch out for his sisters. He still felt protective of all three, so it was hard to keep his mouth shut when he wanted to give advice, such as when Faith had gotten involved in rescue work and when the younger girls had decided to move away. Given a choice, his chauvinistic side would keep them all under glass—at least until they got married and he could hand them over to the next protective male.

Perhaps if he concentrated on his own situation, he wouldn't have the time or energy to obsess over his sisters.

Faith cocked her head to the side and studied him with a serious expression.

"What?" He tried not to squirm. Had she somehow guessed his thoughts?

"So tell me, how is everything with you?" she asked as she examined a scratch on the back of her hand.

He shrugged, not yet ready to voice his interest in Zoe Hart. "Work has been crazy with all the new people in town. You've seen it, too."

"I hear you," she drawled, shaking her head. "The county's resources have been stretched to the max protecting the newbies from themselves." She opened her mouth and then closed it again. "You're trying to distract me."

He struggled to look innocent as she took a drink of her coffee. "I don't know what you're talking about," he blustered.

She always seemed able to smell it when he was being evasive. Now her eyes narrowed suspiciously as she set down the mug. "You've got that goofy grin of a male who's met someone." She wagged her finger at him. "Are you sure it's not one of the nurses?"

Before he could think of an evasive reply, her cell phone rang from inside her purse.

"Sorry." She dug it out and glanced at the screen. The corners of her mouth twitched into a grin before she subdued it, letting Chris know that it certainly wasn't the dispatcher on the other end of the phone.

"Um, mind if I take this?" she asked, blushing as she glanced around the kitchen.

The last thing he needed while in his own single state was to be forced to listen to a mushy conversation between his sister and her new fiancé.

"I need to get the mail." He signaled Ringo with a snap of his fingers. "Tell Cam hello for me."

As Chris walked down the front steps with the dog at his side, the sound of the joy in his sister's voice as she answered her call echoed in his head.

For once the panoramic view from his driveway failed to move him as it usually did. Instead he felt unexpectedly empty and alone.

"See Dr. Taylor in curtain three, Dr. Hart," said the triage nurse when she spotted Zoe. The E.R. was so busy this evening that Dr. Chester had sent Zoe down to help out.

Before she could ask any questions, a woman grabbed the nurse's arm. "I've been waiting for over an hour," she exclaimed forcefully. "I need something for this migraine."

"I understand, Ma'am." The nurse eased free of the woman's grip. "We're doing everything we can to speed things up. If you'll go back to your seat, I'll see if I can find someone."

"I want some attention now!" The woman's voice became shrill, so the nurse herded her back to the waiting area under the security guard's watchful stare.

The woman was still arguing when Zoe walked away. She hadn't gone ten steps when Marty rushed up to her. His red hair was standing on end and his face was shiny with perspiration.

"What are you doing here?" Zoe asked. "Why aren't you in Pediatrics?"

"Three people went home with food poisoning," he replied. "I'm slammed. Got time to check out an old man with stomach cramps?"

"Sorry." She knew what that led to and she wasn't about to fall for Marty's ruse. "Points for the effort, though," she called over her shoulder.

She didn't recognize the officer from the Thunder Canyon Police Department wearing a tan uniform and a heavy green jacket standing outside curtain three. When he saw her, he glanced at her name tag before making eye contact.

"Dr. Taylor called me," she explained. "What's the problem?"

The officer touched his fingers to the brim of his dark

tan Stetson. "Female victim slapped around by her boyfriend. A neighbor called it in when she heard all the yelling."

"Was she assaulted sexually?" Zoe asked.

"She says not, but she's pretty sore. He split her lip and he banged her around pretty good."

Zoe's heart sank. This situation was always a difficult one to handle without letting compassion get in the way of professionalism. Shoving down her deep sense of outrage, she composed her features into an expressionless mask. Before she could enter the cubicle, Chris came out. For once there was no sign of his country-boy grin as he drew both her and the officer away from the curtain.

"Thanks for coming down, Dr. Hart," he said quietly. "We've got a forty-three-year-old woman with a blackened eye and some other visible bruising." His gaze shifted to the officer and then he looked back at Zoe.

"It doesn't sound as though a rape kit is indicated," he continued. "If that changes, see if she'll talk to a counselor from the women's crisis center in Butte and then be sure to have someone call there."

"I'll need to finish my report on Ms. Minsky when you're done," the officer interjected, holding up his clipboard.

"She pressing charges?" Chris asked.

Officer Task shrugged. "If not, we'll have to cut him loose real soon."

"I've got to sew up a prospector's hand, so Carrie will

help you," Chris told Zoe. "Send for me if you need help." For some reason he hesitated. "You okay with this?"

"Of course, Dr. Taylor," Zoe replied calmly even though her insides were churning. She'd handled much worse, but battered women always affected her deeply.

"I'll wait right here," the officer said.

"Someone will get you a chair and a cup of coffee," Chris told him. "Black?"

When he nodded, Zoe saw Chris signal an elderly volunteer, hand him a dollar from the pocket of his scrubs and gesture toward the officer, whose attention had been diverted by a pretty blond nurse. Zoe was impressed by Chris's thoughtfulness in the midst of the chaos going on around them.

As the volunteer headed toward the vending machine, the door from the ambulance entrance burst open and two attendants rushed in with a gurney.

"Dr. Taylor!" called the triage nurse. "Incoming!"

He hurried away without a backward glance and Zoe took a deep breath before entering curtain three.

The cubicle was a small oasis of relative calm within the noise and stress of the department. Carrie stood next to the bed where a woman lay huddled.

"Anna, this is Dr. Hart," Carrie said.

Anna watched Zoe with a wary expression as she cradled her arm gingerly with her other hand. There was dried blood on Anna's cheek, her lip looked swollen and a dark bruise was forming around her eye.

"I don't want a male doctor to examine me," she said, tears threatening to spill over.

Zoe swallowed her frustration. Intellectually she knew this kind of abuse was entirely too common for a number of reasons; emotionally she just plain didn't get it. What part of love inflicted this kind of pain?

"That's all right," she said gently. "Carrie and I will take good care of you, okay?" She glanced at the nurse, recognizing the compassion in her eyes as she reeled off the patient's vitals.

After Chris had sent one patient with internal bleeding to surgery, ordered a battery of tests for another and sent a third up to Radiology for an X-ray, he returned to curtain three to check on Zoe's assault victim.

When Officer Task had first brought Anna Minsky to the E.R., she had been extremely upset, but while Chris talked to her he could see her emotions begin to shut down. Even though Anna had insisted that she hadn't been sexually assaulted, a specially trained volunteer from the closest women's support center had been called. The volunteer would be available in case Anna was interested in hearing about the help and resources that were available to her.

Although Chris had complete trust in Zoe's medical skills, he hadn't observed firsthand her ability to connect with patients on an emotional level. Since he had a moment between crises, it wouldn't hurt to check on both Zoe and poor Anna.

Someone had brought Officer Task a chair as Chris had requested, so he could sit down while he drank his coffee. When Chris pointed toward the cubicle, the officer shook his head.

"The other doc is still in there with her." He tapped the clipboard on his lap. "I'm still waiting to finish my report."

"I'll see what's going on," Chris replied. As he was about to part the curtains, a receptionist rushed up.

"Dr. Taylor, do you have time to take a phone call? It's the pharmaceutical rep from McGraw wanting to make an appointment."

Sales reps were always bringing samples of new drugs and other supplies, a necessary but annoying part of his position as E.R. director. "Get a name and number," he said impatiently. "I'll have to call them back."

When Chris looked into the cubicle, he was surprised to see that Zoe was seated next to the bed holding Anna's hand in both of hers. Anna lay back against the pillow with a large dressing on her cheek.

"How's it going?" he asked when they both looked up.

"I don't think her arm is broken, but I've ordered an X-ray to be sure," Zoe replied. "I explained that a volunteer will be coming in to talk—"

"I don't need a shrink!" Anna exclaimed. "If that cop is still hanging around, you can tell him to leave. All I want is to get the hell out of here."

"Dr. Hart thinks you should have an X-ray," Chris reminded her. "It won't take long."

She sat up in bed and swung her legs to the side. "Look, I appreciate your help, but I'm not some battered wife, okay? I'm not a *victim*. My boyfriend and I had an argument that got a little hot, that's all." She shook back her hair. "Now can I please use a phone to call Bert so's he can come and get me? Pretty please?"

Chris exchanged a glance with Zoe. "You heard her," he said with a sigh. "I'll get Officer Task."

"I'm not pressing charges!" Anna's voice rose. "We'll be fine."

"I hope you're right," Chris said sincerely. "The last thing anyone here wants is to see you come back, because it usually gets worse."

He had seen too many women like Anna. For whatever reason, they didn't or couldn't believe they deserved better treatment than to be slapped or punched, beaten or even raped by the men who claimed to love them.

Discouraged by her refusal to listen, he went to fetch Officer Task. Behind him he could hear Zoe trying to persuade her to wait for the X-ray and the counselor.

Anna wasn't buying either option.

Good luck, he thought grimly. Women like her never seemed to learn. Odds were that she would be back in worse shape than she was now.

Frustrated, Zoe watched Anna follow her boyfriend out of the E.R. Even though he had appeared concerned when he'd come to get her, the look he had given Zoe was chilling, his eyes flat and cold. Not only hadn't he taken Anna's hand, he'd left her to keep up with him as best she could. If she had fainted on the floor, he wouldn't have noticed.

"Ain't he a piece of work?" Carrie asked under her breath as she and Zoe watched the couple disappear. "Too bad the cop was called away before Macho Man showed, or that might have been an interesting meeting."

Zoe was too disheartened to discuss the thug who had picked up Anna. "Did you call the counselor and tell her not to bother?"

"I got her cell," Carrie replied. "Saved her half a trip anyway." She touched Zoe's arm. "Don't let it get to you. Maybe they'll beat the odds and it will work out for them."

Zoe couldn't keep the sarcasm from her voice. "Yeah, he looked real sorry for what he did to her."

"It can be a wake-up call," Carrie replied. "Maybe she'll get lucky."

When the nurse walked away, Zoe looked at the clock and realized that her shift had ended while she'd been with Anna. Inexplicably tired, Zoe went back upstairs for her coat and purse, her thoughts still back in the E.R. Labor and Delivery was fairly quiet and another shift had come on duty, so she was grateful to go home.

Maybe Carrie was right, she thought as she waved at the security guard on duty and went out the front door. Perhaps the boyfriend was really a pussycat despite his tough appearance.

The weather was warmer tonight, giving Zoe hope that spring really had come to Montana after all. She was walking toward the employee lot when she heard the sound of arguing.

The parking lot was empty except for two people standing under a light post. Although they were a couple of rows over, Zoe recognized Anna from the dressing on her face. The man who had picked her up leaned over her, his voice angry, while she pressed herself against the side of an old green pickup truck.

Zoe couldn't help but feel sorry for the woman, even though she couldn't make out what they were arguing about. She hesitated, unsure what to do.

Zoe didn't normally interfere in other people's business, but neither was she able to merely walk away as though she hadn't noticed a potential problem. The parking lot was still deserted and she wished that someone else would either come out of the building or drive up in a car and interrupt them.

Before she could decide what, if anything, to do, the man's voice rose, followed by Anna's cry. Heart lurching, Zoe considered alerting the guard, but he wasn't supposed to leave his post at the front door and she wouldn't want to jeopardize hospital security. She reached for her cell phone, but her fingers touched the pepper-spray canister attached to her key chain. Knowing it was there gave her the impetus she needed, even though she had no intention of actually using it.

"Anna, are you okay?" she called as she walked quickly toward them. "Do you need me to call the guard?" The bully with Anna wouldn't know that Zoe was bluffing.

"She's fine," he shouted back. "No need to call anyone." He said something, voice lowered, as he grabbed Anna's arm and pulled her in front of him.

Zoe slowed her stride, waiting for Anna to respond. Zoe prayed that she wasn't making things worse, biting her lip as she waited and longing for more expertise in knowing what to do.

"I'm okay, Dr. Hart, but thank you for asking." Anna's voice was shaky. "Good night."

Zoe moved closer, trying to see if Anna truly was all right, while the boyfriend stared back at her.

"You heard her. She's just fine," he said, voice bristling with menace as he dropped an arm as thick as a tree trunk across Anna's shoulders.

Zoe half expected her to collapse beneath its weight, but instead she cuddled closer to him. "We got stuff to do, don't we, Doll?" he added. "Private stuff."

Anna's head bobbed like that of a puppet on a string. "Th-that's right," she stammered. When she turned her head, Zoe saw fresh tears on the cheek that wasn't bandaged. Frustration rose in Zoe's throat like bile. "Anna, why don't you come back inside with me," she suggested impulsively. "You don't have to leave—" she'd been about to say *with him* "—right now," she concluded instead. Staring down the boyfriend, Zoe extended her hand. "Come on."

Anna crowded closer to him, shaking her head. "No, that's okay, really. You should go. Bert's taking me home." Her expression seemed to plead with Zoe to not make things worse.

Zoe realized there was nothing more she could do, so she let her arm fall to her side. "Okay, then. Good night."

All the way back across the parking lot to her Honda, she could feel Bert's malevolent stare on her back. Finally she heard two doors slam, followed by the sound of a truck engine firing up. She wanted to look over her shoulder in order to see in which direction he was headed, but she resisted. As the truck roared out of the parking lot with its tires burning rubber, three people came walking out the front door.

At least there would have been witnesses had Bert run her over, Zoe thought grimly as she unlocked her car with hands that shook. She doubted that Anna would have the courage to come forward if he had.

"You off work now?" Vadivu asked Zoe when the two women ran into each other in the employee lounge at the end of their next shift. Vu had been working different hours and Zoe hadn't seen her for several days.

Zoe managed a smile as she lounged back in her chair. Worrying about a patient was usually an exercise in frustration, but she couldn't help wondering how Anna was doing. If she did end up coming back to the E.R., Zoe probably wouldn't even hear.

"Yes, I'm off work, thank goodness," she answered Vadivu. "I'm tired and starved. Want to get a bite somewhere?"

A fleeting frown marred the other woman's honey-toned complexion. "Aren't you coming to the pub?" she asked. "Everyone's headed over there to celebrate St. Patrick's Day."

"I didn't know you were Catholic," Zoe teased, which earned her another puzzled look from the Indian girl.

"I'm not, but why do you ask me that?"

"Never mind, I was just kidding." Zoe's only concession to the occasion had been to wear a pair of small, apple-shaped earrings made of green jade. She'd had to point to them more than once today to avoid getting pinched by an overzealous intern.

Vadivu folded her arms, obviously waiting for a reply to her question about the pub.

"I don't think I could face all that crazed merriment," Zoe said. "Thanks anyway."

"No, you must come with me," the other girl insisted, grabbing Zoe's wrist. "You live alone, you don't come over to the parties at the apartment. You're too much of a recluse, so it will be good for you to get out with people."

She gave Zoe's arm a tug. "I will not take excuses.

Besides, they're serving green beer." She leaned closer, lowering her voice, and gave a delicate shudder. "And corned beef if you are willing to eat that sort of thing, which I am not."

Swilling down beer of any color and eating pub food with a bunch of loud, tipsy hospital workers didn't sound the least bit appealing to Zoe, but she figured it would be easier—and quicker—to stop in for a few moments rather than continuing to argue. Besides, being included felt rather nice.

"Okay, okay," Zoe said with a smile as she gently disengaged her wrist. "Just let me fix my hair first." She pulled out the pins anchoring it in a loose knot and shook it free. "You want to ride with me?" she asked, digging her brush from her purse.

Vadivu was applying dark red gloss to her full lips. "Yes, please," she replied when she was done. "Now hurry up, or all the best seats will already be taken."

Chapter Six

When Chris finally got to the dimly lit pub, it was already filled to overflowing with customers, including a number of hospital workers, all intent on celebrating the holiday properly. Loud Irish music poured from the sound system as green beer flowed from the taps.

While Chris stood in the doorway checking out the crowd, an obviously tipsy lab tech saluted him with a half-full mug, sloshing some on the floor. A middle-aged nurse from the clinic who stood in the crush at the bar gave him a warm smile that he returned with a wink. Several other people smiled and waved. Thunder Canyon might be full of recent arrivals, but there were no strangers on St. Paddy's Day in an Irish pub.

The paneled walls were decorated with swags of green bunting and paper shamrocks. Matching balloons and silver streamers dangled from the ceiling while the mingled aromas of corned beef and cabbage permeated the air like perfume, reminding Chris that he had skipped lunch. The afternoon's cases had included a critical heart infarction, a child with a crayon stuck up her nose, a family with food poisoning and a pair of combatants in need of stitches because of an earlier bar fight down the street.

"Hey, Doc Taylor!" The head of the hospital accounting department, seated at a corner table, held up a pitcher of beer like a trophy. With him were a couple of board members and several other doctors, one of whom beckoned to Chris.

Chris returned his wave, but he could see that every chair at the table was taken. Most of the other tables and booths were full, as was every seat at the bar. People stood elbow to elbow, juggling glasses and plates of food as they shouted over the lively fiddle music. Waitresses in green blouses and short black skirts carried full trays through the crowd.

Someone handed Chris a schooner of beer, which he drained in several long, thirsty gulps while he listened to a couple of miners argue about the basketball playoffs. The beer sloshed into his empty stomach, bringing with it a pleasant buzz and a faint warning to eat something before seeking a refill. Friendly people kept stopping him to say hello, which slowed his progress toward the pool table that had been covered with a white cloth for the occasion.

"Dr. Taylor! Over here!"

He looked around to see Barb signaling wildly from a booth where she sat with several other residents, including Zoe and Vadivu. Peter was donning his coat, preparing to leave, so Chris lifted his glass high to avoid getting it knocked from his hand as he changed direction.

"Thank you!" he exclaimed when he reached the booth and Barb slid over to make room for him. "Hello, all."

During the chorus of greetings, Barb topped off his glass. He caught Zoe's eye and smiled across the cluttered table. A rush of warmth coursed through him that had nothing to do with green beer or the heat generated by the crowd of bodies. For a nanosecond, the impulse to lean over the table and kiss her seemed like a dandy idea.

No more booze on an empty stomach!

With great reluctance, he got back to his feet. "Will someone save my seat?" he asked. "If I don't eat something, I'm liable to start dancing a jig on the tabletop."

"By the saints, that would be a sight to see," replied Marty in a phony Irish brogue that earned him laughter all around and an elbow in the side from Barb.

Chris wanted to ask Zoe if she would still be here when he got back, but his sensible side knew better than to single her out in front of her co-workers. To his delight, she touched Marty's arm.

"Let me out, will you?" she asked. "I want to get some cake before it's gone."

As she walked with Chris to the buffet table, the crowd parted for her like the Red Sea in a biblical epic. She seemed oblivious to the admiring glances she received from many of the males she passed, but she was probably used to getting attention from men.

Chris tore his gaze away long enough to exchange hellos with a group of nurses, but he didn't stop. He noticed Caleb Douglas holding court at a round table near the middle of the room, where the mayor and the chief of police appeared to be hanging on to his every word. They were probably discussing the mine or the ski resort. According to the gossip, Caleb had been running short of funds until his illegitimate son had shown up. His intention had been to ruin Caleb, but he had ended up investing in the ski resort instead.

Caleb probably didn't need Justin's money any longer, as long as there was no truth to the rumor about the missing deed to the Queen of Hearts. A loud burst of laughter from Caleb's table seemed to prove that the wealthy businessman didn't have a care in the world.

As Chris walked by, Caleb got to his feet and opened his arms to a pair of new arrivals.

"Hello, Son," he bellowed over the noise, hugging first Justin and then his new bride, Katie, the town librarian.

During the town's Heritage Day celebration, the couple had been married in what was supposed to have been a fake wedding. Afterwards they'd been trapped together during a blizzard. Now their happy expressions and Justin's possessive arm around Katie's waist, anchoring her close, indicated that there was nothing fake about their feelings for each other.

"Are those the newlyweds?" Zoe asked curiously, stopping next to Chris.

"Sure are." He felt a pang of envy at their obvious happiness. "Can't you feel the heat?"

For a moment her face looked wistful, but then she raised her eyebrows as she handed him a plate. "It must be nice to own a gold mine."

Zoe's comment made him wonder if she had financial concerns of her own despite her new car and the apartment in a building that was nicer than hospital staff housing. Perhaps her folks were threatening to turn off the money tap.

"That's only a part of the Douglas family holdings," he replied, helping himself to corned beef, cabbage and boiled potatoes. "Is everything okay?"

She selected a small square of chocolate cake with green frosting. "Fine, thanks. And you?"

"Better now that I've seen you," he replied.

She flashed him a grin. "I suppose a bit of blarney is normal, considering what day it is," she responded drily before she walked away toward their booth.

Chris realized that he stared after her with a sappy grin on his face. He glanced around to see if anyone had noticed, but they were all busy having too good a time to pay any attention to one lovesick idiot with drool on his chin.

When he got back to the booth, a couple more of the residents had left. Vadivu and Barb got up and grabbed their purses.

"We're going down the street," Barb said to Zoe. "Do you want to come with us?"

Zoe shook her head. "Thanks anyway, but I'm going home as soon as I finish my cake." She poked at it with her fork. "Do you need a ride?"

Vadivu shook her head. "Thanks, but we're going with a couple of the interns," she replied, shrugging into her coat. "I'm sorry to desert you two. Will you be okay?"

"She'll be fine," Chris replied with a grin as he slid onto the bench opposite Zoe. He wasn't sorry that the other girls were leaving. "I'll watch out for her."

Vadivu seemed to hesitate, but then Barb grabbed her arm. "Come on," she said. "They're waiting by the door and I don't want them to leave without us."

"Go," Zoe said. "I've got my car."

With a last wave, the two girls hurried away. Chris was relieved. He'd been concerned that Barb might have a little crush on him, but obviously she just liked to flirt.

Zoe shifted to the far end of the booth where she concentrated on the cake in front of her as though she were performing a heart transplant.

Chris scooted down so that he was sitting across

from her, hoping for a few moments of privacy before someone took advantage of the empty seats. As people had begun trickling out of the pub, newcomers kept replacing them, so the joint remained busy.

"Would you like some coffee or tea with that?" he asked.

Her expression softened. "No, but thanks for asking."

Chris stared at the curve of her mouth. Its shape fascinated him. He didn't normally go around lusting after every pretty woman he saw, but something about Zoe had registered high on his lust meter since he'd first seen her strutting down the corridor in her doctor's garb with her stethoscope hanging around her neck.

He tried to focus on that physical attraction and to ignore the signs of strain on her face, but looking after people who needed a little tending was too deeply ingrained.

"How are you really?" he asked in a low voice as he broke a soda biscuit in two and spread butter on half. The food in front of him had suddenly lost its appeal.

She looked up again, her expression guarded, before returning her attention to her plate. She cut the cake into small meticulously even squares and then stabbed one of them with her fork. "I'm fine."

The rich sound of a bow being drawn across the strings of a fiddle sliced through the buzz of conversation. Applause greeted the bearded man standing in front of the bar wearing green suspenders with his work clothes.

Chris and Zoe were both silent as the fiddler played a lively tune with speed and skill. As he urged his audience to clap along with him, two couples got up to dance.

Under the cover of the music, Chris slid aside his unfinished plate and leaned across the table.

"Something's on your mind," he guessed. "Are you thinking about one of your patients?"

"I treat lots of patients." She thrust out her chin in a gesture that was becoming all too familiar. "Is there a problem with something I did?" she demanded.

"No, of course not." He reached out to pat her hand, just as he might do with one of his sisters. The only trouble was that touching Zoe gave him a distinctly unbrotherly reaction. "It's okay to care about your patients," he said, "as long as you focus on the things you can treat and don't get overwhelmed by those you can't."

She pulled back her hand. "What makes women like Anna put up with that kind of abuse?" she asked sadly.

Chris let out a sigh of frustration as the fiddle player switched to a ballad. The clapping died quickly as he continued to play.

"Damned if I know," Chris admitted. "I suppose she's looking for someone special, just like the rest of us."

If his personal admission registered, Zoe didn't let on. "Do you think Anna will be all right?"

He couldn't very well lie. "If she won't accept help,

there's not much we can do," he replied. "It's possible that what happened to her was an isolated incident, an argument that got out of control."

Biting her lip, Zoe shook her head. "I saw the two of them in the hospital parking lot after the man who assaulted her picked her up." A frown pleated Zoe's forehead. "She seemed…intimidated by him."

Chris didn't know what to say. "Let's hope we don't see her again in the E.R."

Zoe pressed her lips together firmly as she set her crumpled napkin next to her half-eaten cake. "You're right, Dr. Taylor. It's frustrating, but that's all we can do."

He hadn't meant for their conversation to take such a depressing turn, especially when everyone around them seemed to be having such a good time.

"I thought we'd gotten past the formality, *Zoe.*" He tried not to let his frustration show. "You should know that you can talk to me about anything and I'll try to help."

The annoyance in Chris's tone startled her. He was just trying to be understanding, and she had retaliated by throwing up her usual defensive wall. It wasn't his fault that she was struggling against her attraction toward him.

"I'm s-sorry," she stammered, taking the coward's way out. "I guess I'm tired. It's been a long day."

He slid to the edge of the bench. "Let me take you home."

"But you haven't finished," she protested, glancing at his half-full plate. "While I was talking your ear off, your food got cold."

He flashed the grin that she found increasingly difficult to resist. "I wasn't that hungry."

Before she could think of a reply to his obvious fib, a couple walked up. Zoe recognized the woman, a pretty blonde, from all the publicity surrounding the rescue at the mine. Her resemblance to her brother was unmistakable and the man with her looked vaguely familiar, as well.

"Hey, bro," the woman said to Chris as she leaned down to kiss his cheek. "Sorry to interrupt, but there's nowhere else to sit." She included Zoe with a smiling glance. "Okay if we join you?"

Chris made room next to him on the bench. "This is my bratty sister, Faith," he told Zoe, "and her fiancé, Cam Stevenson." He reached up to shake Cam's hand. "This is Zoe Hart from the Golden State."

Faith stared at Zoe, making her wonder if she had green frosting smeared across her teeth. "Nice to meet you," Faith said as she sat down next to Chris and Cam joined Zoe.

Zoe studied Chris and his sister curiously. Good looks must run in the Taylor family. With her big hazel eyes and blond hair a shade lighter than her brother's, Faith was as stunning as Chris.

They appeared to be so easy with each other, their affection obvious. What would it be like to have some-

one who knew you almost as well as you knew yourself, but still cared for you?

Zoe couldn't begin to guess.

"Do you work at the hospital, too?" Faith asked her
after Cam had ordered a pitcher of beer from a passing
waitress.

"Zoe's an OB/GYN resident," Chris explained before she could answer.

"You must be homesick," Faith observed.

Again Chris spoke up. "We keep her too busy for that."

"How do you like Montana?" Faith asked persistently.

"What is this, twenty questions?" he demanded.
"Give her a break."

Faith turned to frown at him. "You didn't mention
that the poor woman was mute."

"I'm not," Zoe said, looking at Chris. "I think Dr.
Taylor is just in the habit of taking charge, but I'm per-
fectly capable of speaking for myself when I'm allowed the opportunity."

The waitress set a full pitcher of beer and two more
glasses on the table. Cam's wallet hand was faster than
Chris's. He handed her several bills.

"You go, girl," Faith told Zoe as Chris poured their
beer. "It's about time someone put my bossy big-deal
brother in his place." Eyes twinkling, she raised her
hand, palm outward in a salute.

As she and Zoe exchanged a high five, Cam snorted
with laughter. He was an attractive man whose appear-

ance hadn't drawn a spark of reaction from Zoe, even before she'd noticed the adoring way he gazed at Faith or the ring that sparkled on her finger.

"Hey, I thought men were supposed to stick together," Chris protested. It was obvious that he was attempting to appear outraged, but the humor in his eyes gave him away.

Cam spread his hands in a gesture of innocence. "Sorry, buddy. When I'm with two gorgeous women, there's no way I'll side with another guy."

The banter helped to relax Zoe. "I'll take that as a compliment," she replied, turning to grin at Cam.

From the corner of her eye, she saw Chris's smile fade. He couldn't be jealous, so he must not like her being friendly with his sister's fiancé.

"That's a beautiful ring," Zoe said pointedly.

Faith's pride was obvious as she stuck out her hand.

"It's very unusual," Zoe said. The round yellow diamond was surrounded by smaller white stones, like a sun with its rays. "Did you design it?"

Faith touched the ring affectionately. "It was Cam's idea."

Zoe had seen many lovely pieces of jewelry in the shops along Rodeo Drive, but none of them could outshine such a loving tribute. "It's beautiful."

"You must miss your family," Faith said. "Are they back in California?"

Zoe knew that Faith was just making polite conversation. "I do miss my parents, of course," she replied. "But we e-mail and I talk to them on the phone."

The other couple appeared to be interested as they sipped their beer. "I really enjoy working at the hospital," Zoe continued. "You're lucky to have such a modern facility."

"Especially here in Podunkville," Chris interjected, earning a frown from Faith, who jabbed him with her elbow.

Zoe didn't voice her agreement with his comment. "I feel very lucky to work with Dr. Chester in Labor and Delivery," she added diplomatically, lobbing the conversation back to Faith. "Do you know her?"

"We've met, although I have to confess that hospitals aren't my favorite places," Faith replied.

"Wasn't Olivia the reason you came to Montana for your residency?" Chris asked Zoe.

"I was wondering what brought you here when there must be so many facilities closer to home," Cam remarked.

"I heard her speak at Berkeley when I was going to medical school," Zoe explained. "I admire her work a great deal."

"Thunder Canyon has to be a change for you," Faith said. "Are you adjusting okay?"

Zoe wasn't willing to deny the truth. "I must admit that there are things I miss about L.A.," she admitted, trying to be tactful. "I guess I'm a city girl at heart."

Chris's brows rose like two golden arches. "The smog, the crime, the traffic?" he guessed.

"The culture, the amenities, the civilization," she countered. "Sorry. I guess defending my hometown is a knee-jerk reaction."

"Zoe, have you had the chance to do much sightseeing yet?" Cam asked, turning to face her. "I'm from Denver and I thought I'd seen the best that Mother Nature had to offer, but I have to say that the scenery around T.C. is really wonderful."

Zoe attempted to appear regretful. "Between work and studying, I haven't had much free time."

"Are you working tomorrow afternoon?" Faith asked.

Zoe hesitated, unwilling to be caught telling an outright fib in case Chris happened to check the schedule. "I'm not sure," she hedged. "I don't think so."

"Great!" Faith exclaimed, clapping her hands. "We're taking Cam's son, Erik, ice-skating after school. You can come with us."

"Ice-skating?" Zoe echoed. Her mother had made sure that her education included piano lessons and gymnastics. She'd taken skating lessons, too, until it became clear that she possessed neither the talent nor the drive of an Olympic contender.

"It will be fun," Faith insisted, reaching across the table to grab Zoe's hand. "Have you ever skated at an outdoor rink?"

Zoe had to laugh. "Not in Southern California!"

"Come with us," Cam chimed in. "I'd love for you to meet Erik. He's a great kid."

Chris hadn't said a word. Perhaps he didn't care for the idea of her getting to know his sister.

"I don't know," Zoe mumbled, wishing she were able to read his expression.

"I need feminine support," Faith urged, squeezing her hand before letting it go. "I won't take no for an answer unless you have to work."

Chris finally spoke up. "Zoe's a beach bunny. She wimped out at the snowball fight at my place and I'll bet she can't skate." He leaned toward her with a challenging expression. "Afraid of looking ridiculous?" he challenged. "I'll bet you can't even stand on blades."

"Snowball fight?" Faith echoed. "When was that?"

Chris waved his hand in a dismissive gesture. "Not important."

There was no mistaking the gauntlet he'd tossed down. Wouldn't he be surprised when she skated circles around him?

"If you really want me to go, I'll give it a try," she told Faith. "Thanks for asking me."

When Chris arrived at the Gold Medal Ice Arena the next afternoon, he recalled his sister's comment the night before.

"You owe me, Topher," Faith had murmured with a sly grin before he'd left the pub on Zoe's heels.

From his very first crush on Patsy McGee back in

fourth grade, his sister had always been able to tell with laser-point accuracy whenever he had the hots for a girl. His only hope was that maturity and Faith's own blossoming feelings for Cameron Stevenson had lessened her enjoyment in Chris's discomfort.

Now as he parked in the gravel lot, he was glad the weather had been cold enough to keep the outdoor rink open. Once the temperature grew too warm, the couple who owned the rink would close up until fall and hit the road in their RV.

Chris got out of his car, hooking his old hockey skates over his shoulder, and looked around for Zoe and his sister. He didn't see them, but the rink was busy for a weekday. He'd called a neighbor whose son was always happy to earn extra spending money by feeding Chris's stock when he got held up.

The covered warm-up shack was doing a brisk business renting skates, and customers were already lined up at the snack bar. Nothing much had changed since he was a kid. Colored lights were strung between poles that surrounded the frozen oval and music poured from the speakers.

On the ice, a chunky woman in sweats blew on a whistle to signal the end of a figure-skating class. Half a dozen little girls in short skirts and mittens glided like ducklings to the exit, where their parents waited patiently on hard wooden benches. As soon as the ice was empty, a teenage boy drove an ancient Zamboni out to resurface it for the upcoming session. Chris still remembered the name of its inventor, Frank Zamboni, from a school report he'd once written.

"Hey, Chris! Chris!"

He turned to see Cam's son, who was seven, waving wildly as he ran toward Chris, carrying brand new hockey skates. Walking behind Erik were his dad and the two women. Chris recognized Zoe instantly in her purple jacket as she and Faith chatted like old friends.

When Zoe burst out laughing, an icy finger of nervousness ran down his spine and he prayed that some unflattering story about him wasn't the source of her amusement. He relaxed again when Erik reached him. As much as Faith enjoyed teasing Chris, she would never willingly hurt him.

"Hey, buddy." Chris reached down to ruffle Erik's straight auburn hair. "Where did you get the new skates?"

"My dad bought 'em," Erik replied, almost dancing with excitement.

Chris was relieved to see no permanent effects from Erik's ordeal of being trapped in the abandoned mine.

"Aren't they cool?" he demanded, holding up the skates. "We got them at Faith's store."

She worked part-time at her friend's store, Extension Sports, when she wasn't busy rescuing people.

"Way cool," Chris agreed, patting his own beat-up skate boot. "I'm jealous."

After losing his wife in a car accident when Erik was only four, Cam had been understandably afraid that something might happen to his son, too. Unfortunately, he'd been overprotective of Erik to the point of smothering him.

Since the rescue, Cam seemed to be making a real effort to loosen up. Maybe he had come to realize that protecting Erik from every possible danger in life just wasn't possible. Or maybe falling for Faith had made Cam a believer in second chances—as it had her.

As Erik spotted a schoolmate and rushed over to show off his skates, Chris turned to wait for Zoe, who was picking her way across the gravel in sexy, high-heeled boots. Along with her fur-trimmed parka and knit cap, she wore a black turtleneck sweater and matching jeans that hugged her long legs.

In the general chorus of hellos, he managed to touch her shoulder. She returned his wink with a cool smile, but he wanted to think that her rosy cheeks were because of him and not the chilled air.

Even in the unforgiving afternoon light, her skin looked flawless. Her only makeup appeared to be a smudge of something to darken her eyelids and a sheen of gloss slicked across her full lips.

Chris let the other three go ahead of him in line at the ticket booth while he hung back with her. "I'm glad you came," he said quietly, letting his gaze play over her face. "You look gorgeous."

"Thank you." Her stare made him wish he'd worn something more trendy than his tan suede jacket, plaid flannel shirt and blue jeans. What would a hip

California sophisticate wear? He realized that he had no clue.

"What do you think of Erik?" he asked as the line shuffled forward. "He's changed a lot from the timid little boy he was when I first met him."

She watched him hopping impatiently from one foot to the other. "It sounds like his dad's engagement to your sister has been good for him," she said quietly.

Chris wanted to tell her why Erik was so good for Faith, as well, but the information wasn't his to share. Throat suddenly tight with unexpected emotion, he had to swallow hard as the line moved again.

"Your sister seems very nice," Zoe added after a moment. "I told her I'd meet them here, but she wouldn't listen."

"Faith seldom listens to me, either," he replied. The pleasure of being with Zoe coursed through him like the effects of a fine old brandy. "When it comes to my sister, sometimes it's just easier to go with the flow."

Zoe shrugged. "That's hard for me," she admitted as he took out his wallet. "I guess I'm more comfortable being in control."

"A smart person knows when to take charge and when to let it go." He took out enough money for both their tickets.

"Did you read that in a fortune cookie?" she asked, unzipping the fanny pack she wore around her waist.

Ignoring her question, Chris paid for two tickets and handed one to her.

"That's not necessary," she protested, holding up the line. "I'll pay my own way."

He took her elbow and urged her forward. "Remember what I said," he told her. "Sometimes it's better to just go with the flow."

Her eyes widened, but then she shrugged as an older woman standing behind them started to giggle. "And don't argue when someone else offers to pay," she exclaimed.

Zoe hesitated, but then she followed Chris through the gate. "Double or nothing on who falls first once we get on the ice," she told him with a wide smile.

Chapter Seven

Zoe had accepted Faith Taylor's invitation because she needed a break from work. At least that was what she had told herself until she got out of Cam's SUV and saw Chris waiting for them.

Even now, as she waited for his reaction, awareness flowed through her like an electrical charge.

"Double or nothing on the first one to fall?" he repeated. "Sure you can afford to take the risk?"

She was on thin ice in more ways than one. "Count your money, Hotshot," she replied. "I'm not the one risking anything."

"We'll see about that," he replied as he extended his gloved hand. "Deal."

As they walked to the covered building next to the open-air rink, he leaned back to look at her from behind.

"What are you doing?" she demanded, twisting around so they were still facing each other.

"No pillow, so maybe you know how to keep your balance," he observed with a gleam in his eyes. "No fair pulling me down with you when you fall."

Zoe realized that for once she didn't feel the usual pressure to do a good job and avoid embarrassment at all costs. Except for their silly bet, no one here expected anything from her; no one was judging her performance.

"I guess you'll have to wait and see how I do," she said with a sassy smile. "I hope they have decent rentals."

"You should buy a pair," Chris advised. "Faith can get you a discount at the sporting-goods store where she works."

"It's a little late in the season," Zoe replied, more interested in buying a new bikini for the beach back home than investing in winter sports gear.

She indicated the battered skates that were slung over his broad shoulder. "Those look like something you stole off a broken-down hockey player."

He held them up by the laces. "Maybe that's my alter ego."

By the time Zoe had gotten her skates from the rental room and finished lacing them up over two pairs of socks, Faith and Cam had followed Erik onto the fresh ice. Cam didn't appear to have much more experience than his son.

At the edge of the ice, Chris extended his hand to Zoe. "Once around before we start the wager."

"Okay." When she felt the firmness of his grip, her only regret was the gloves they both wore. The touch of his skin against hers would have been worth a few frostbitten fingers.

"Doing okay?" he asked after she had taken a few cautious strokes on the ice without stumbling.

She glanced up, biting her lip with concentration. "I think so."

"Take your time," he said. "It's not like we're going anywhere."

Up ahead, Erik skated between Faith and Cam, his ankles wobbling from side to side as he clung to their hands. Cam looked shaky, too. When Erik fell, pulling Faith down with him, Cam struggled to help them up. Instead he fell down, too, as all three of them laughed.

"Maybe we should have bet on them instead of each other," Chris commented as he skated effortlessly on his straight hockey blades.

"Rich doctors like you shouldn't try to make money off poor hardworking residents like me," Zoe retorted.

"Who said that I'm rich?" he demanded. "Your car is newer than mine."

She swerved to avoid another skater. "It's leased," she replied. "Where did you learn to skate?"

"I played a lot of hockey on the frozen ponds around here when I was a kid." He glanced down at her feet. "You're doing fine."

"Glad to hear it." With a sudden laugh, she pulled her hand free and pushed off with her toe pick. "You're it!" she cried, tagging his arm as she streaked away.

The wind blew against her face, cooling her flushed cheeks as she darted easily around other skaters, changing edges as she went. From behind her, she heard his shout of surprise.

"You'll be sorry!" he called. "The bet's still on."

From the corner of her eye, Zoe saw Faith's startled glance and Cam's thumbs-up sign as she executed a neat turn so she could keep an eye on Chris. There was plenty of room to maneuver and he was gaining on her fast. She hadn't considered that a game of tag was more suited to his skating skills than her own, but at the last second she dodged his outstretched hand and changed direction. It took him a moment to recover and follow. With a pirate's grin on his face and the wind ruffling his hair like greedy fingers counting pieces of eight, he bent low and power stroked, cutting her off at an angle.

This time when she changed direction, ducking around three giggling girls, Zoe found herself trapped at the railing behind two little boys. She turned back around just as Chris caught up with her. Bracketing her between his hands on the railing, he looked into her eyes with their bodies nearly touching.

His hair was a halo in the sunlight and his complexion was ruddy. "This demands a forfeit."

Zoe stared up at him, mesmerized. If he took her in his arms right here, she might not have objected, but a chaste kiss was certainly more appropriate.

"Okay." She rose up on the toes of her skates, intent on doing just that.

Before she could touch her mouth to his cheek, he startled her by shifting his hands to her shoulders, stopping her. "Oh, no, you don't."

Zoe's jaw dropped, followed immediately by a burning rush of humiliation when she saw his unsmiling expression. How had she misread him so drastically?

She tried to twist away from his grip, but she had nowhere to go. If she attempted to go around him, her body would rub against his.

Taking his hand from her shoulder, he tucked his finger under her chin and gently tipped back her head. From behind him, someone emitted a low whistle.

"I want a rain check," Chris said.

"A what?" Zoe asked blankly. If he'd made a pass when she was at the local bar, she would have known exactly how to shut him down. Her own sudden awareness of him, however, was almost more than she knew how to handle.

For a moment, she was transfixed as she stared up at him.

"I'm willing to wait," Chris said, his voice husky.

He released her in time for a shouted warning to

make them both turn, as Erik, arms flailing, smacked into the railing. When Chris reached out to steady him, Erik accidentally kicked his blade and they both went down.

Zoe bent over them. "You lose," she told Chris, and then she helped Erik back up.

"Sorry," he said. "I lost control."

"There seems to be a lot of that going around," Chris drawled as he got to his feet and brushed the ice from his jeans. "Who wants hot chocolate?"

In addition to losing his bet with Zoe, it had cost Chris another twenty bucks for Cam to tell Zoe that he couldn't drop her off, after all. Glancing at Zoe seated next to him in his car, Chris figured he had gotten off cheap.

"Where do you live?" he asked, even though he knew the answer. He had recognized the address when he'd reviewed her file, but he didn't think it would be wise to mention that a former girlfriend had lived in the building.

Zoe gave him directions and then fell silent as she removed her knit gloves. The only sound in his "preowned" Beemer came from the stereo. He'd been right when he'd said her car was newer than his, but he wasn't a slave to appearances.

Yanking off her hat, she tossed her head and fluffed up her hair with her fingers, well aware of his glances. Hands gripping the steering wheel in a stranglehold, he hoped she couldn't hear his heart thumping against his chest.

After they had finished their cocoa, they'd gone back out on the ice as darkness had fallen around them. All he could think about was getting her alone and claiming his forfeit. Whether that made him a flaming romantic or an immature, oversexed idiot, he wasn't sure. All he knew was that his normal cool-guy, easygoing persona had temporarily deserted him.

She shifted in the leather seat next to him. To his disappointment, she had declined his invitation to stop for pizza, claiming that she needed to review a procedure for tomorrow.

As they drove down the main street, he cleared his throat and broke the silence that was beginning to border on painfully awkward.

"Where do you learn to skate like that?" he asked. How inane the question sounded to his ears, like a preteen pickup line.

"My mother believes in raising a well-rounded offspring," Zoe replied, her tone brittle. "When I wasn't in school, I took lessons."

"What kind of lessons?" he asked curiously as he slowed for a turn and drove past a row of small older homes with their windows lit up. The only lessons he'd ever taken were to play his mother's piano. What a waste of money that endeavor had been!

"You name it," she replied, gazing straight ahead. "Music, singing and ballet, followed by tennis and swimming when I got older."

"So you're a woman of many talents," he ventured.

"Or one who has few talents to discover."

Her self-derisive comment shocked him. At first impression, she seemed to be brimming with confidence. But he was beginning to realize that was a facade.

"You're a good doctor," he said firmly. "In my book, that beats earning an ice-dancing medal any day of the week."

It was Zoe's turn to look surprised in the soft glow from the dash. "But you told me that I could be better," she reminded him.

"There's always room for improvement, which is what you've definitely done." He slowed the car as they approached her building. "To the point where you've got to watch that you don't get overly concerned over Anna Minsky." He touched her hand. "Lighten up, Zoe. You're doing fine."

She didn't say a word as he parked the car in front of her apartment.

"Let me get your door and then I'll walk you up," he said firmly.

He half expected her to bolt from the car instead of waiting, but she didn't.

"I'm not inviting you in," she warned as he held open her door and extended his hand.

"And I'm not asking." His reply was deliberately provocative in order to distract her from their recent conversation.

Predictably she turned away, the heels of her boots tapping on the pavement as she led the way to her apartment. Hands in the pockets of his jeans, Chris sauntered along behind her, relieved to notice that the walkways were well-lit and the shrubs were trimmed back. With all the new arrivals in Thunder Canyon, security was bound to become a bigger issue than in the past.

When she reached her front door, she turned to face him. "Thank you for the ride," she said politely. "And for—"

He braced his hand on the wall next to her head and leaned closer. Even with her heels, he topped her by several inches.

"My forfeit," he whispered, prepared for a chaste kiss on the cheek.

If she had shown the slightest sign of reluctance, he would have backed off faster than a cow pony with a slack rope. Instead, she caught him by surprise by sliding her arms around his neck and tipping back her head.

Chris didn't need directions to figure out his next move. He had been waiting for a long time to satisfy his curiosity about the feel and flavor of her tempting lips, but he wasn't about to be stampeded into rushing the moment. With hunger burning through him like moonshine, he cupped her face in hands that weren't quite steady.

Knowing that Chris wanted to kiss her sent a shiver of excitement through Zoe. She could read his hunger in his narrowed eyes and in the flush that stained his cheekbones, could feel the tension in the way his fingers tightened on her scalp.

For a moment she let herself savor the warm melting sensation that flowed through her when she pressed against him, the strength of his arms when they tightened around her, pulling her even closer—and the passionate reaction to her nearness that he didn't bother to hide.

When she lifted her head and smiled invitingly, she expected him to plunder her mouth. Instead, he leaned down slowly, his steady gaze on hers and his breath on her face, until she wanted to moan with frustration. When her knees went weak, she realized that somehow she had lost control of the moment, helplessly following his lead. Before she could figure out what had happened, he finally touched his mouth to hers.

Warmth seemed to start at that single point of contact, mouth on mouth, and spread through her entire body. She felt him smile against her lips before he pulled back and stroked them with his tongue. Finally, as she forgot to breathe, he slipped inside.

A husky groan came from deep in his throat. A tremor went through her as she buried her fingers in the warm silk of his hair and angled her head to slide her tongue against his, and then to kiss him with growing impatience. He pressed her against the wall and ravaged her mouth as they battled each other for control.

Somewhere in the dim recesses of her overheated mind, Zoe became aware that this easygoing country doctor had managed what far more sophisticated males had failed to do. He had shattered her defenses and stirred a response from her that she was more than eager to give.

Finally, inevitably, he ended the kiss so they could both regain their breath. Chest heaving against her hand, he held her with his cheek against her hair and let out a wry chuckle.

"Honey, you've got a bag of surprises behind those cool blue eyes." His voice was husky. "My brain's melted, my knees are fused and I think my heart needs a jump start to get it going again."

Lifting his head, he tucked a strand of hair behind her ear and let his fingertips trail down her cheek. "I sure as heck know that I've never felt anything as good in my life as our first kiss," he added.

His sweet words and the slightly dazed look in his eyes warmed her, despite the chill of the evening air. She didn't care that he must be exaggerating. Surely an attractive doctor like Chris had been with plenty of women during school in Chicago and here in Lightning Gulch. Even so, his silly, over-the-top comment broached the normal awkwardness that she might have felt after sharing such an overwhelming embrace.

"In that case," she whispered, sliding her hands up the front of his jacket as she watched him through narrowed eyes, "the second kiss will burn down this building."

He angled his head. "Call the fire department, because we're about to find out."

His lips were a breath away from hers when the door

to the next apartment opened abruptly. Automatically Zoe sprang away from him to see her middle-aged neighbor blinking at them owlishly through his thick glasses. He was wearing an overcoat and his face turned an unhealthy shade of red.

"Uh, good evening," he muttered. "I didn't mean to, uh, interrupt…uh, sorry." Ducking his head, he hurried away.

Face burning, Zoe stared silently until he had disappeared around the corner.

"Mr. Gale, my high school biology teacher," Chris muttered, stuffing his hands into his pockets. "He told me once that I was too girl-crazy to ever amount to anything."

Zoe looked at Chris's blank expression. Something gave way inside her and she let out a whoop of helpless laughter as she collapsed against her door. "He was right!" she gasped.

For an instant, surprise flashed across Chris's face and then he, too, began to laugh. Helplessly Zoe tried without success to regain her composure because each time she started to wind down, one look at Chris sent her into a fresh eruption of giggles. Unable to stop, they fell into each other's arms. Finally Zoe pulled away. With a stitch in her side and tears streaming down her cheeks, she was able to get her breath.

"What a way to ruin the mood," she exclaimed, fanning her face with her hands. She couldn't remember the last time she had laughed so hysterically.

Blushing, Chris returned her grin. "Sad, but true."

Lightly he tapped the end of her nose with his finger. "Rain check?"

Feeling as though she had been put through an emotional wringer, Zoe experienced a rush of relief that he wasn't going to push the situation. Before she took another step, she needed the chance to figure out where she was headed.

"I had a good time," she said politely as she dug out her key. "And thanks again for the ride home."

A muscle flexed along his jaw. "Don't blame Cam for bailing on you," he said, speaking rapidly. "I paid him."

Zoe frowned, confused. "He said he had to get home and let the dog out before it piddled on the carpet."

"Cam doesn't have a dog. I gave him twenty bucks to tell you that."

"I don't think anyone has ever done that for me before," she admitted, stunned by his confession. "I hope the kiss was worth it."

"Every penny." There wasn't a shred of doubt in his voice.

What could she possibly say—that she was pleased to hear it? "Good night, then."

Still slightly dazed, she went inside and shut the door, locking it carefully before she fell back against it on legs that trembled. When she closed her eyes, she could still feel the tingle of his mouth touching hers.

After a frustrating night, Chris's day off work began with a call from his younger sister, Hope, who shared an apartment in Missoula with his youngest sister, Jill. Although Hope had a decent job with an insurance company, she was always short of funds.

"I'm two months behind on my Visa payment," she told him tearfully. "I hate to ask, but the dentist bill took all my spare cash. Could I borrow some money?"

Chris raked a hand through his hair, doing his best to keep the frustration from his voice. "I thought you paid off your credit card with the money I sent you in January."

"I needed a new coat." Her voice iced over. "What did you expect, for me to get pneumonia? Would you rather get stuck paying big fat medical bills while my credit goes into the toilet?"

Eyes closed, he shook his head.

"I don't know why I call you." She rushed on while he silently counted to ten. "You're just like Dad."

"Hope," Chris interrupted quietly, trying to head off the worst of the tirade.

Her voice ratcheted up a notch. "I don't know why I bother asking for help. You want me to fail so I'll have to move back home and live under your thumb."

No way! Chris pinched the bridge of his nose. "I've offered to help you draw up a budget," he said when she paused for breath.

"That would be wonderful," she replied, switching direction again with the abruptness of a quick-change artist. "I promise, as soon as I get caught up on everything, I'll take you up on that. I really, really will this time."

He'd heard it all before, he thought as her voice droned on like the whine of a mosquito in his ear. Hope was looking for a handout, not advice. No doubt she'd hit up their folks for help before calling him. Either she hadn't been able to reach them or they'd gotten tougher and turned her down this time.

Chris glanced at the clock. They were probably out on the golf course.

"How much is it that you need?" he asked abruptly, interrupting her stream of empty promises.

"What?" Obviously his capitulation had caught her off guard, but she recovered quickly, naming an amount he knew was higher than her first request.

"I'll send you a check." Where had he gone wrong? "How's Jill? Is she there?" He refrained from pointing out that they seldom called unless they needed something.

"Um, no," Hope replied, sounding rushed now that she had gotten what she wanted. "Jill had an early class, but I'll tell her hi for you."

"Listen," he said, shifting the phone to his other ear. "About that budget—"

"Can we talk about it later?" she asked. "If I don't get in the shower right this minute, I'm going to be late for work." She laughed lightly. "You don't want me to get fired, do you?"

"What I want is to help you get back on track," he said, but he already knew he was talking to himself.

"I know, I know," she chanted. "Could you send the check today?"

"Sure thing. I'll pick some cash off the money tree out back." He heard the sound of running water in the background.

"Gotta go. Love and kisses," she said. "Bye."

Before he could reply, the connection went dead. Muttering a couple of choice words, he slammed down the receiver and headed for the bathroom.

After he'd dressed and completed his morning chores, he returned to the house. Pacing the kitchen like a caged lion, he reached for the phone a dozen times before changing his mind. Twice he nearly tripped over Ringo as the dog followed him anxiously.

"Dammit!" Chris's exasperation finally poured out. "Go lay down!"

Ears flattened to his head, tail drooping, Ringo slunk away to crouch beneath the dining room table.

Instantly Chris felt a wave of remorse. He had no right to take his frustration out on man's best friend.

He bent over and peered at Ringo. "Jeez, I'm sorry."

Head resting on his paws, Ringo didn't move.

Getting down on all fours, Chris crawled under the table and extended his hand. It took several moments of coaxing, but the dog finally relented and gave it a halfhearted lick.

Feeling only slightly better, Chris backed out the way he had come and got to his feet. He walked over to the front window and stared at the view without seeing a thing.

He couldn't very well call Labor and Delivery in the

vague hope of catching Zoe between patients. Leaving a message that he couldn't wait to see her again would be equally ineffective—except perhaps to fuel the hospital gossip mill. Besides, what could he say to her— *were you as shaken by that kiss as I was? Did you lie awake and think about me?* Questions like those were guaranteed to spook her like a skittish horse in a fireworks factory.

Totally frustrated, he grabbed the phone and called Faith to see if she had plans, but she had been summoned to the other end of the county. His calf-roping buddies were busy, the stock was all fed and the stalls were clean. He had intended on pushing the vacuum while he dealt with the laundry, but the sky was too clear, the air too clean and he was too damned restless to stay indoors. Finally he thought of Willie.

An hour later, the retired bull rider showed up with his saddle loaded into the back of his old pickup truck. Together they worked Denver and another of Chris's Quarter Horses. Eventually the mounts began to tire, so the men unsaddled, cooled and brushed them before turning them out.

"How about a cold one?" Chris asked.

Willie's weathered face creased into a smile. "Sounds great."

Since Chris was technically on call, he grabbed a beer for Willie and a soda for himself from the small fridge in the tack room. As they nursed their drinks, they leaned against the fence and watched the horses graze.

"Denver's coming along," Willie commented between swallows. "You going to try him out?"

Chris took a hefty swig of his cola. "I figured on hitting a couple of the smaller shows first," he replied, referring to the scattering of weekend rodeos held in neighboring towns. Amateur riders like Chris competed in every event from calf roping and steer wrestling to racing barrels and busting broncs. Some did it for the experience, with the hope of moving up to bigger shows and bigger purses. Others, like Chris, just liked to compete.

"What else is new with you?" Willie asked casually.

When Chris looked at him from the corner of his eye, Willie stared straight ahead, as if mesmerized by the sight of grazing horses.

The two men had been friends for a long time, but Chris had been raised to work things out himself while he looked out for everyone else, not to ask for advice in how to run his life. As he tipped back his head and swallowed the last of his soda, the impulse to confide in Willie passed.

"Nothing much happening," Chris said as he bent to pat Ringo. "How about you? Heard from your sister lately?"

"She may come out this summer." Willie pushed back the brim of his battered Stetson. "Florida gets muggy and she's looking for a break."

Chris was about to reply when the cell phone clipped to his belt signaled a call from the E.R. Excusing himself, he answered.

"Dr. Taylor, I hate to ask on your day off," said the triage nurse, speaking quickly, "but we're short-staffed due to a conference in Butte. A woman with possible internal injuries from a beating was just brought in and two victims of a car accident are on their way. Can you come?"

A bolt of intuition shivered through him. "The woman, what's her name?" he asked.

Hoping he was wrong, he listened to the nurse shuffle papers.

"Anna Minsky."

His fingers tightened on the cell phone. "I'll be right there. Meanwhile see if Dr. Hart is up in Labor and Delivery. She'd want to know about Anna."

Chapter Eight

"You look hot today, Doc." The middle-aged lab tech's gaze settled a few inches below Zoe's face as he stepped in front of her, blocking her path and slowing her headlong departure from the hospital at the end of her shift.

Her hand itched to slap away his smirk, but she knew better than to let him provoke her. She settled for a contemptuous glare as she went around him. If she didn't get out of here *now*, she was going to lose it.

"Stuck-up," he muttered just loud enough for her to hear as she walked away.

Moments later, she passed the security guard, waving her hand in acknowledgment before bolting through the front doors. The lump in her throat was so big that it threatened to choke her. Her vision blurred and her stomach churned as she hurried across the empty parking lot. Silently she prayed to reach her car without running into anyone she knew.

She kept hearing the pleading in Anna Minsky's voice before she'd been wheeled up to surgery with internal bleeding.

"It was my fault," Anna had whispered to Zoe. "He didn't mean it."

Zoe knew that Anna wouldn't press charges, nor would she talk to a counselor. The next time—and there would be a next time—Anna's journey might take her directly to the morgue.

With a gasp of relief, Zoe reached her car. She hit the remote, fumbled open the door and almost fell into the front seat. She beat her hands against the steering wheel to vent some of her frustration, but then a car drove by and the driver gave her a startled look. Feeling slightly foolish, she took several deep, steadying breaths as she stared unseeing through the windshield.

For once Zoe regretted not living with the other residents, because it would be nice to go home and talk shop. She thought about stopping at the pub to see if anyone she knew was there, but the idea of walking in alone was too distasteful.

If she went back to her apartment feeling so churned up, she would never be able to sleep tonight. She considered trying to find Vadivu, or even Barb, gave Chris a brief, longing thought and then dug her cell phone from her bag. She owed her mother a call and she really needed to hear a caring voice.

Patrice answered on the first ring. "Hi, Baby. How are you?" As usual, her voice sounded rushed, as though she was urging Zoe to hurry up and get to the point. "I'm on my way out the door for a meeting," she said. "Is everything okay?"

"Of course," Zoe replied automatically. "But I—"

"I was starting to worry, since I haven't heard from you in so long," her mother interrupted. "You must be really, really busy."

Guilt flushed through Zoe, even though she sent regular e-mails. "I'm sorry," she replied. "My hours are so irregular and you're hard to catch."

"So it's my fault?" Patrice asked, voice rising. "I see. I'll try harder to be available for you even though I'm working hard to pay for the rent on your apartment and the car."

"I didn't ask for either of them," Zoe protested without thinking. Damn. Now she sounded ungrateful.

The silence on the line sent a fresh knot of tension to her stomach as she tried desperately to figure out where she had gone wrong.

"I'm sorry," she began again, but her apology was interrupted by an audible sigh.

"I just want you to be safe," Patrice said softly. "Is that so wrong?"

"No, of course not. I do appreciate everything," Zoe insisted. "I just called because—"

"So your work is going well?" Her mother's tone had brightened.

"Pretty much," Zoe agreed. "I had this patient tonight, though—"

"Baby, I hate to interrupt, but I have to meet a client," Patrice said. "He wants a second look at a listing in Bel Air. You know what that means."

"Big commission," Zoe replied. "I understand. Well, good luck."

"Thanks, Baby. I'll let you know if they buy it. Gotta run. Kiss, kiss."

Before Zoe could say goodbye, the line went dead. Biting her lip, she glanced at the luminous face of her watch. Her father would be home by now, his cell phone turned off. She dialed his other number, hoping his new wife didn't answer.

After three rings, there was a click and a message began in the voice of a very young child. Zoe's half brother, Marcus. Part of the way through his stumbling, too-cute recitation of their phone number, Zoe gave up in disgust. At least if she drove home, she could write a couple of e-mails on her laptop. Perhaps then she might feel better.

Zoe hadn't noticed anyone following her out of the hospital lot, but another vehicle pulled in behind her when she parked in front of her building. In the bright glow of the headlights, all she could make out was a truck with one person inside.

Half the people in town drove pickup trucks.

Perhaps it was a stalker, she thought on a wave of grim humor as she got out of her car, purse held firmly in one hand and front door key in the other. She could tell *him* about her crappy day.

As she glanced behind her, the headlights went out abruptly. It would probably serve her flip attitude right if she *was* being followed. A shiver of nerves ran through her. She wasn't really crazy enough to hope for a confrontation with a stranger just because she was frustrated.

With the strap of her purse over her shoulder, she got out of her car, set the alarm and wrapped her fingers around the pepper-spray container in her coat pocket. Her other hand was curled into a fist with her door key protruding between two fingers like a weapon as she hurried down the path to her unit.

"Zoe, wait. It's just me."

She turned to see Chris standing by his truck. Gulping in a deep breath, she let go of the pepper spray and uncurled her fist.

"I'm sorry about Anna," he said, coming to a stop on the pathway a dozen feet from her as though he wasn't sure of his welcome. "I saw you leave work, so I just wanted to make sure that you're all right."

Something inside her that had been wound so tight she had feared it might pull apart gave way abruptly.

With it came a flood of emotion she hadn't even realized she'd been holding back since her last glimpse of Anna's gurney disappearing into the elevator.

Zoe heard a sob. She was shocked to realize the harsh sound had come from her. As she crammed her knuckles against her lips to stop their trembling, Chris opened his arms.

Without hesitation, Zoe bolted. When she reached him, throwing her arms around his neck, he enfolded her in a hug that nearly lifted her off her feet. She pressed her face against the front of his jacket, too relieved to speak.

"It's okay," he whispered into her hair, swaying gently back and forth as he held her tight. "Shh. It's okay now."

She melted against him, soaking up his warmth. Under her cheek, she could feel the reassuring beat of his heart.

"How did you know to come?" she choked.

His chest expanded when he drew in another breath. "Call it doctor's intuition."

She looked into his eyes, as dark as the faraway ocean. "Will you come in?" she asked. "I don't want to be alone." It was a huge admission for her to make, but she was afraid he might leave.

Except for a slight tightening of his arms, he didn't react.

"You need me to listen?" he asked. "I'm good at that."

"I *need* you," she repeated helplessly. "Not to listen."

"You're vulnerable right now," he argued as though he knew her better than she did herself, but she could feel his reaction as she snuggled against him. He, too, was vulnerable, but in an entirely different way.

If she didn't find an outlet for the emotions roiling inside her, she was going to explode. Impatiently she jerked away from him. "I know what I want and it's not a willing ear."

A muscle flexed in his cheek. He tipped up her chin with his fingers, studying her through narrowed eyes. Something in her face must have convinced him, because he leaned down and pressed his mouth to hers in a brief, hard kiss.

"Okay, then. I'm your man." His voice was harsh. Bending down, he scooped her into his arms and carried her effortlessly toward her unit.

"Someone might see us," she said without really caring. "Everyone knows you."

"My reputation with Mr. Gale is already shot," he countered. "I've got nothing else to lose. How about you? Worried?"

"Not a bit." At least not about the neighbors, but she wasn't too sure about her feelings.

The moment he got her inside the apartment, kicking the door shut behind him, she pulled his head down for another heated kiss. This time it lasted until they were both breathless.

Chest heaving, he let her slide down his aroused body until she stood on her own shaky legs. Face flushed, gaze locked on hers in the faint light from the street, he peeled off his jacket and let it drop to the floor while she did the same. After another passionate embrace, she grabbed his hand and led him to her bedroom. Here, too, the blinds failed to block all the light from outside. The bed and the other pieces of furniture were faintly visible.

The working part of her brain was glad she had left the room neat and the bed made when she'd left for work this morning, but the rest of her just wanted him naked as quickly as possible.

He kissed her again, cupping her face in his hands. She tugged the hem of his shirt free of his jeans and skimmed her palms up his ribs, exploring the lean muscle and warm skin. He reacted with a sharp intake of breath. When she fumbled with the big unfamiliar buckle, he brushed aside her hands in order to pull her sweater over her head.

"You're gorgeous," he breathed, stroking her through the lace of her bra.

Her nipples drew into hard buds and heat curled in her stomach. "It's too dark for you to see me," she protested, kicking off her shoes.

"Turn on the lamp," he whispered.

Instead she switched on a night-light near the door. It gave off a faint pink glow. Then she toyed with the zipper of her jeans, smiling when he reached for her impatiently.

He bent his head to string hot wet kisses across her

shoulder and down her cleavage. When he undid the front clasp of her bra and covered her breasts with his hands, his touch sent a lightning bolt of reaction through her. Desperate for more, she skimmed her fingers around his waist inside the band of his jeans, making his stomach muscles quiver.

Letting go of her, he sat on the bed and removed his boots while he watched her peel off her jeans and her socks. Reaching into his pocket, he set a small packet on the nightstand. She was pleased that he was being responsible.

In a moment, they were both nearly naked. Swallowing hard, she stared at his wide chest and muscular build, at his dark snug-fitting shorts.

"Last chance to say no." His voice was deeper, thicker than usual.

Her answer was to cup him lightly through the fabric. He reached around her to strip the bedspread and blankets from the bed. Then he pushed her gently down and followed her.

As he covered her body with his, she wrapped her legs around him and they rolled back and forth across the mattress. He stripped off her panties while she tugged at his shorts. With their hands and mouths they stroked and tasted, explored and caressed, as she struggled to hang on to her control and shatter his. Finally he planted a knee between her thighs.

"Look at me, Zoe," he said firmly.

Open and helpless, she glared her resentment.

Slowly, expertly, he caressed her until she shattered with a sob.

He allowed her to turn the tables, but only for a moment. Muscles trembling, he dragged her back up the bed. Sheathing himself quickly, he tipped up her hips and slid into her.

"Yes, please," she urged, pressing closer. "Yes, yes, *yes!*"

He rode her hard until the sound of his name on her lips broke his control. He felt her tremors. With a hoarse groan, he threw back his head and surrendered.

When Chris woke up, the room was still in shadows. He hadn't meant to fall asleep when he'd finally pulled the covers over the two of them. His arm was still curled around Zoe, tucking her close. She fit against him like his other half, her breathing deep and slow. He hated disturbing her, so maybe he would wait for a few more moments before he got up.

She had a right to be tired, he thought with a purely masculine smirk. They had worn each other out. Vaguely he recalled falling facedown on the mattress, limbs leaden, finally too exhausted to lift his head. He had figured on a nap and gone into a coma, instead.

As good as it felt to hold her, he shouldn't stay. With a twinge of regret, he tried to shift his arm without disturbing her. His watch had gone the way of his clothes, ending up on top of a dresser on the far side of the room.

He turned to look at the clock on the nightstand next to him, startled when he saw the time.

It was far later than he had figured.

Zoe turned and her eyes blinked open. Doctors learned early the ability to come awake in an instant.

"Hi," he whispered, propping his head up with his bent arm.

"Mmm," she replied, stretching like a cat. When she arched her back, the sheet slid down to reveal her perfect breasts. The darker tips beaded in the cool air, begging his attention.

Chris swallowed hard. Until this instant, he would have bet on his body being too satiated to respond to anything short of a cattle prod, but he would have been wrong. It was a struggle not to roll over and slide between her thighs, claiming her again before he left.

Knowing the packet he always carried with him was empty stopped him like a cold shower. Being prepared was a habit, like brushing his teeth, but he hadn't planned for a sexual marathon.

Nor had he figured on spending the night, so his truck was parked right on the street in front of her unit like a big red arrow, in case anyone cared to look. Despite that, he was almost unbearably tempted to stay. But staying longer could eventually erode his good sense. He wasn't made of stone.

"Sorry," he muttered, "I didn't mean to wake you."

She tugged up the sheet. "I'm a light sleeper."

He couldn't see her face clearly enough to read her expression. "Are you all right?" he asked softly.

She made no move to touch him. "Of course. I'm a big girl."

You certainly are might get his face slapped, so he merely leaned down to kiss her forehead. "I'd better go," he said softly.

Immediately she sat up, all business, with the sheet pressed against her. "If you want to shower, I can make coffee."

He would have preferred that she shower with him and the hell with the coffee, but he knew that wouldn't be wise, so he grabbed the excuse to stay a little longer as though she had tossed him a life ring.

"That would be great, thank you." He hated being so damned polite after the intimacies they had shared. He knew her body almost as well as *Gray's Anatomy,* at least by touch.

Frowning, he flipped aside the covers and got to his feet. "You sure you don't mind?"

She gave no indication that her night vision worked on his nude body. "The bathroom's that way," she said as she switched on a small lamp by the bed. "There are extra towels in the cupboard." Giving him one last delicious peek, she reached for a nightshirt draped over a nearby chair and slipped it over her head.

It was like tossing a tarp over a brand-new Porsche. Some works of art weren't meant to be covered.

She looked startled when he walked determinedly

around the bed, instead of heading for the bathroom, but she didn't resist when he put his arms around her.

"You know what I just figured out?" he asked.

She stiffened slightly. "What?"

"How good this feels." Drawing her against him, he rested his cheek on her hair. She smelled womanly and sweet. "I could hold you like this until my arms fall off."

For a moment, she relaxed against him, making him resent the damned nightshirt even more.

"And I'd let you," she murmured against his chest. "Then we'd both get fired."

Relief eased the knot in his gut, followed by a bubble of pleasure that put a grin on his face. "Naw," he drawled. "I know people."

"Important people?" she asked. "Ones who could save our jobs?"

He couldn't resist the urge to tease her. "Well, mine anyway."

"Rat!" She pulled out of his arms and slapped his bare buttock hard enough to make him yelp.

"That hurt." As he rubbed his burning cheek, she was nearly out the door. Below her hem, her legs went on forever.

"Get moving!" she ordered over her shoulder. "And don't use all the hot water."

When he came out of the bedroom a few minutes later, fully dressed except for his boots, she was seated at the small kitchen table in a long blue robe and matching slippers. What he had seen of the compact apartment was scrupulously neat and about as personalized as a room at the Butte Best Western.

In addition to a pot of coffee, she had fixed him a stack of toast. "Would you like some eggs?" she asked, sliding back her chair.

"No, thanks. This is great." Feeling less vulnerable to temptation now that he was dressed, Chris leaned down and kissed her the way he had wanted to since he'd first opened his eyes. He reluctantly broke it off in order to breathe.

"What about you?" he asked. "Are you going to eat? Have you eaten?"

"It's the middle of the night," she reminded him. "How do you like your coffee?"

He picked up a piece of toast, suddenly hungry. "Black, thanks."

She busied herself at the counter while he wondered whether she had grown up with household help. It made him realize how little he knew about her—besides the fact that she liked being on top. Her preference for the dominant position didn't surprise him one bit.

She set two coffee mugs on the table, followed by a napkin, a knife and a fancy-looking jar of blackberry jam.

He wished he knew what she was thinking when she sat back down across from him, but her face was unreadable when she propped her chin on her hand.

"Are you working in the morning?" he asked, feeling guilty for keeping her up so late.

"I'll be fine," she replied as he sipped the hot coffee. "Do you always try so hard to look after everyone else?"

He pondered that while he spread jam on a slice of toast. "I suppose so. That was the way I was raised. Dad worked a lot, so when Mom was busy it fell to me to look after my sisters." He took a bite, remembering his last frustrating phone call from Hope. If only she would listen to him!

"I've often wondered what it would be like to have brothers and sisters," Zoe mused, fiddling with the handle of her mug. "Well, I have a half brother, but he's only four and I don't see very much of him."

Chris lifted his eyebrows. "That must be difficult for you."

Zoe frowned down at her hands. "Marcus was born just a few months after my parents' separation. As soon as their divorce was final, my father married Marcus's mother. She used to work for him."

"How's your mom?" Chris couldn't imagine his parents getting a divorce, but who ever could? "Is she okay?"

Zoe rolled her eyes. "She's a workaholic, so I doubt she's had a lot of time to miss him. Or me," she added, her tone slightly bitter.

"The two of you aren't close?" he probed.

Looking uncomfortable, Zoe took another sip of coffee. "I've disappointed her." This time her voice was so low that Chris barely heard her.

For a moment, he thought he'd misunderstood. "Disappointed her?" he echoed, stunned. "How could you?" He waved his hand. "You're a bright, beautiful, accomplished woman. Any parent would be proud of you." He realized that his voice had risen, so he took a deep breath to calm himself.

"Well, thank you." Zoe looked away, clearly uncomfortable. "You haven't met my mother. Patrice is a hard act to follow, believe me."

"In addition to being a fine doctor, you can skate circles around the local hockey protégé," he added with a grin. "Is she aware of *that?*"

Zoe shook her head, but she, too, had started to smile. "I'll be sure to tell her."

Chris felt a surge of tenderness. No wonder he'd seen glimpses of vulnerability beneath the confidence she wore as though it were a suit of armor.

When he patted her hand, he noticed the time on his watch. "Damn, I'd better go," he said reluctantly. "Thanks for the coffee."

When he got to his feet, she did, as well, with her arms wrapped around herself protectively. He wanted to carry her right back to bed and cuddle her close.

"I meant everything I said just now," he blurted, touching her shoulders lightly and feeling her tension. "You're a very special woman in more ways than you suspect."

He hoped she might say something in return, giving him some clue to her feelings about him and what they had shared. Instead she bit her lip and glanced away. "Thank you."

Disappointed, he let her go and perched on the edge of the nondescript tweed couch to pull on his boots. When he got back up, she held out his jacket. After he'd put it on, she reached up to adjust his lapel.

Chris leaned down to kiss the tip of her nose. "Lock the door after me," he said gruffly. "And get some sleep. I'll see you at work."

"Aye, aye, sir," she drawled, but at least she was smiling when she closed the door behind him.

What the hell had she been thinking? Zoe demanded silently after Chris left. Arms wrapped around herself, she paced the length of her living room. She knew better than to get involved with someone on staff, but when she got near him she didn't seem able to think at all.

From outside, she heard his truck start up. After he drove away, the sound fading into the silence of the night, a wave of longing shivered through her.

When he kissed her, she felt it down to her toes. He reeked of sex appeal and when he——

Heat flashed through her when she recalled what they had done together as she'd lost herself in his arms. He was a passionate and generous lover who held nothing back and seemed to expect no more than her full surrender in return. The passion they shared was intoxicating, but her vulnerability when she felt herself spinning out of control was scary as hell.

Chapter Nine

Zoe was used to functioning on very little sleep, so fatigue wasn't much of a problem at work the next day. Neither, she reminded herself several times an hour, was the distraction of daydreaming about Chris.

Because of a bad rainstorm that had blown through town right after she arrived at the hospital, causing several auto accidents, the E.R. was busy. It wasn't until midmorning when she was between patients that her cell phone rang. She checked the screen, glanced around furtively and ducked into an empty supply room.

"I've only got a minute," Chris said after they had exchanged hellos. "It's crazy down here." His deep voice sent a shiver of reaction along her nerve endings.

"I've been hearing sirens all morning." She was breathless, as though she had just finished running up the stairs. "Anything interesting come in?"

"Just the usual mayhem," he drawled, "but no criticals so far." His tone became more intimate. "Do you have any idea how difficult it was to leave you last night? I wish someone needed a consult so that I could see your face, hear your voice for a minute. It would keep me going for a few more hours."

His comment made her go hot all over. "I have responsibilities," she said, struggling for lightness. "It's not like I'm sitting around buffing my nails while I wait to be summoned by the king of the E.R."

"King?" he sputtered. "How about emperor?"

"Oh, right." She glanced at her watch. "In fact I've got two women in labor as we speak and I'm expecting Dr. Codwell in a little while."

"Listen, about later—" he said. Through the phone, she heard a sudden commotion and shouting. "I'll call you back," he exclaimed and then he was gone.

She didn't hear from him again all day, nor was she called down to the E.R. before the end of her shift. Before she left, she went to the surgical department to check on Anna.

The television was on, but the woman's eyes were closed. The bruise on her cheekbone was fading. Studying her from the doorway, Zoe felt a surge of frustration. When she noticed the huge vase of flowers on the windowsill, she wanted to throw it at the wall.

She was about to leave when Anna opened her eyes. "Dr. Hart," she exclaimed, her face brightening as she pushed the button to raise the head of the bed. "I wasn't asleep."

"How are you feeling?" Zoe asked.

"I'm doing okay. But…they had to take out one of my ovaries." Anna sounded tired. "I'm getting out later, but I have to be careful for a couple of weeks." A shadow crossed her thin face. "Thank you for coming by. You must be awfully busy."

"Not too busy to check on you," Zoe replied briskly. When she glanced at the bed table, she noticed a flyer lying there from a women's support center in Butte.

Anna must have noticed the direction of Zoe's gaze. "A woman came by this morning. She made me realize that Bert's not going to change."

"Unfortunately that's usually the case," Zoe agreed carefully. "All too often, the violence escalates."

Anna sighed and her eyes filled with tears. "That's what Ruth said when she helped me fill out the complaint against him."

Stunned by her news, Zoe reached for the box of tissues and handed it to her. "Good for you," Zoe said, as Anna blotted her eyes. "You did the right thing."

Anna glanced at the flowers. "He'll be mad that he wasted his money on those."

Bert was going to be very angry and not just about the flowers, Zoe thought. "What are your plans?" she asked.

"My sister's packing up my stuff while Bert's at work. I'm going to stay with her in Spokane for a while. That's where I'm from."

Zoe leaned down to pat the other woman's shoulder. "You'll be fine," she said. "You're stronger than you think, so good luck."

"You're the reason that I talked to Ruth," Anna blurted before Zoe could turn away. "I wanted you to know that."

Zoe's puzzlement must have shown on her face. "I don't understand."

"Do you remember that night out in the parking lot?" Anna asked. "It made me realize that even a stranger was more concerned about me than I was about myself, and certainly more than Bert."

Zoe was stunned. "Thank you for telling me. That's nice to know." With a last quick smile, she fled from the room, fighting sudden tears of her own.

She had made a difference, she thought as she hurried down the corridor, blinking rapidly until she regained control. Elation filled her and she could hardly wait to tell Chris.

She checked her phone for messages before she left work, annoyed by her sharp pang of disappointment that the only missed call was from her father. He would never understand why she felt so good about Anna. He thought Zoe should have gone into plastic surgery.

That's where the money is, he had said more than once. She'd call him back later, when she was ready to listen to his latest Marcus stories.

As Zoe drove back to her apartment, exhaustion from the night before finally began to sneak up on her. Following Chris's departure, she had gone back to bed, but she hadn't slept well. A garbage truck had woken her at dawn, so she'd gone down to the exercise room to work out before coming to the hospital.

Maybe a microwave dinner and an early night wasn't a bad idea. She needed to keep her priorities straight.

Despite what had happened with Chris, they weren't exclusive, weren't in a relationship and, technically, they weren't even seeing each other.

For all she knew, she realized with a tight feeling in her midsection, he might be seeing someone else…or a whole flock of someones, although Zoe hadn't heard any rumors to that effect on the grapevine.

What she needed to remember was that she had no idea just what, if anything, was going on with him except that it was, by necessity, only temporary. From the time she first arrived in Thunder Canyon, with its too-cutesy Western theme and small-town minds, she had been counting the months until she could kick the dust from her shoes and move on with her life.

On the other hand, Chris's life was rooted here. No question of that. If things had been different and a choice needed to be made, he would *hate* L.A. Worse yet, she didn't think he could survive there. For all his good qualities, he didn't have the savvy or the survival skills—the L.A. *edge.*

Out of the sack, sweet and sexy Dr. Taylor just wasn't aggressive enough—not for Beverly Hills and certainly not for Zoe. Not long-term.

She was halfway home, feeling better for having worked it all out in her head, when her phone finally rang. She glanced at the screen and pulled over to the curb, feeling a spurt of excitement despite the direction of her thoughts.

"Hey, how was your day?" Chris asked.

"Exhausting," she replied around a huge yawn. "I think I'm crashing after the adrenaline rush." She was tempted to tell him about Anna, then decided to save it until she saw him in person. "How about you?"

"If I think about why you're tired, I'll drive off the road." His voice had gotten husky, sending heat spiraling through her. "Look, I just got out of a meeting with a sales rep and I forgot that I'd already promised to have dinner with Faith and Cam."

Zoe knew a brush-off when she heard one, but she was still disappointed.

"That's okay—" she began.

"It's nothing fancy," he continued, "just casual dress at The Hitching Post. Come with us? I want to see you."

Another yawn overtook her before she could answer. Priorities, she reminded herself, ignoring temptation. She had a full schedule tomorrow.

"I can't." She didn't bother to hide her regret. "I've got some book work."

"What if I stop in after you've had a chance to study?" he suggested. "I can test you."

She knew what would happen if he showed up. What she needed was distance, not a repeat of the night before.

"I don't think that's a good idea," she said as she watched the passing cars through her window. "Rain check?"

"Sure," he said agreeably. "Maybe later in the week would be better for both of us."

She frowned, disappointed that he had given up so easily, then shook her head at her own ambivalence. What did she want from him? That was something she needed to figure out.

"Thanks for understanding," she said quietly. "Tell your sister and her fiancé hello for me."

"Will do. Get some rest."

Before she could decide whether to tell him about Anna after all, he rang off, leaving her to stare at the rain hitting her windshield. As she pulled back onto the street, she wondered why she felt so frustrated. Hadn't she gotten exactly what she'd wanted?

During work the next day, Zoe kept her personal thoughts at bay. At midmorning, she checked the sutures from a patient's hysterectomy. A knock on the door caused both her and Beth Ann, the nurse assisting her, to look up as Dr. Chester poked her head into the room.

"Excuse me, Dr. Hart," she said. "Would you please come see me when you're done here? I'll be in my office."

"Of course," Zoe replied, her stomach dropping like a stone at the sight of her superior's serious expression.

"Sorry for the interruption," Dr. Chester told the patient, a woman in her forties.

After the doctor left, Zoe and Beth Ann, who was dressed as usual in a smock printed with teddy bears, exchanged significant glances. Beth shrugged. Although she couldn't very well comment in front of a patient, her wink said, *No big deal.*

"I hope you aren't in trouble," the patient said, her expression apprehensive.

Zoe made a notation on her chart before responding. "I certainly hope not." She kept her tone even, wishing she could be as confident as she must sound. "You're healing nicely and the scar will fade in time."

After a brief exchange, Zoe wrote up a prescription for a mild painkiller. Excusing herself, she left Beth Ann to finish up.

As Zoe walked down the hallway with its pastel wall-paper border, she reviewed the possible reasons for her summons. Had she overlooked something or made a mistake in procedure? Misdiagnosed a patient's condition?

Maybe that cranky old Mrs. Morel had complained

about Zoe's attitude. The woman certainly hadn't been happy when Zoe had advised her to quit smoking if she intended staying on the Pill. Or perhaps the young girl Zoe had treated a couple of days ago—Wanda something—had taken offense to Zoe's lecture about her high-risk activities. If Wanda—no, *Wendy,* that was it— didn't make some changes, she was headed straight toward contraction of an STD or HIV.

Zoe hesitated outside Dr. Chester's office, sucking in a deep breath before she knocked on the door frame.

The director glanced up over the top of her reading glasses, then made a welcoming motion. "Come in, Doctor." She flipped a file folder closed. "Sit, please."

Obediently Zoe took the chair facing the desk, crossing her legs as she tried to interpret the other doctor's smile.

"Tea?" Dr. Chester offered. On a small side table, a pot of water sat on a hot plate next to a woven basket filled with herbal tea bags.

Zoe's system was already humming along on caffeine. "No, thanks."

She waited, braced for the worst, as the doctor removed her glasses and let them dangle from a beaded cord around her neck.

"How are you adjusting to small-town life here in Thunder Canyon?" Dr. Chester asked, folding her hands. "It must seem very different from what you're used to. Have you settled in all right?"

Zoe admired her supervisor a great deal, but until

now their conversations had always been about work. "I'm doing fine, thank you." Mind racing, she kept a mildly inquisitive expression plastered on her face. When she realized that she had allowed her hands to curl into fists, she flattened them against the fabric of her skirt.

The director seemed to be waiting for more. "It's a nice town," Zoe added lamely.

"Not like California, though," Dr. Chester said with a nod of understanding. "You must miss your family."

Zoe searched for potential land mines. An affirmative reply might make her appear too dependent, but *no* seemed too emotionally detached.

"Sometimes, I guess." Indecisive, unable to make decisions. Great. "They're pretty busy, but my laptop and e-mail make it easy to stay in touch," Zoe added.

For a long moment, Dr. Chester studied her silently while the nerves in Zoe's stomach jumped like fish in a net and she struggled not to fidget. Finally the older woman sat back in her chair with her deeply tanned hands folded in front of her. They were unadorned except for the turquoise ring she always wore.

"Have you thought about what you might do once you've completed your residency?" she asked.

It took Zoe a moment to click over from the dire possibilities circling her brain like tiny thunderclouds. Hastily she bit back the first reply that came to mind, *Beat feet back to L.A.,* and scrambled for something a bit more diplomatic.

"I haven't planned that far ahead," she said, trying to be tactful.

"Have you given any thought to remaining here in Thunder Canyon?" Dr. Chester asked. "This town is in desperate need of more physicians who specialize in women's health."

Zoe swallowed a bubble of incredulous laughter. "I hadn't really considered it."

"Of course it's no secret that Dr. Codwell is getting older," Dr. Chester continued. "If he should decide to slow down, he might need an associate to share his patient load." Absently she touched her earring, a small silver hoop. "This is in no way official, you understand. He's not said anything to me."

"I see." Zoe was reluctant to say more in case she had misunderstood Dr. Chester's intention. Maybe she was just making conversation. Besides, Zoe had never seriously considered practicing medicine anywhere except L.A. Somehow she couldn't envision her parents bragging about their daughter, the Montana doctor.

"The gold strike is attracting a lot of people to this area, including women who must have access to specialized health care," Dr. Chester continued. "When the new ski resort opens, the need will become critical. We'll need a facility just for women."

Zoe knew she should say something. "I suppose that's true." God, she sounded like an idiot! Clearing her throat, she tried again. "Some of the patients I see could go to a women's clinic instead. It would certainly ease our patient load."

"So you see, there will be plenty of career opportunities in our community for bright young doctors." Dr. Chester's dark eyes seemed to twinkle as she leaned forward. "I hope you'll think about staying on. According to the reports I've been getting, your people skills have come a long way since you first arrived."

Zoe supposed that she owed Chris for bringing the weakness to her attention. "Thank you," she said, flustered by the praise. "Your opinion means a great deal to me."

"I wouldn't have the slightest problem in giving you a glowing recommendation." Dr. Chester tapped her own chest with her fingertips. "You have a good heart, but you're afraid to believe in yourself. Until you do, Doctor, true satisfaction will elude you, and not just in your career." A shadow crossed her face. "Believe me, I speak from experience."

Zoe wasn't sure how to respond. "You've given me a lot to think about," she said finally.

With a nod, the other doctor slipped her glasses back on, signaling an end to their conversation. "I won't keep you any longer. Just remember that words can only hurt you if you let them."

After Zoe had thanked her again, she excused herself and left the office, puzzling over Dr. Chester's parting comment as she headed back to the main station. As she passed the supply room, Beth Ann came out with an armload of fresh blankets and towels.

"Is everything okay?" she asked softly, her eyes filled with concern.

"Yes, everything is fine," Zoe replied. "Couldn't be better." A good recommendation from Dr. Chester would be crucial, especially since Zoe had no clue as to what Chris might do.

"Well, it's nice to see you smiling," Beth Ann replied. "Good luck with, um, with everything." Cheeks turning pink as though she was flustered, she hugged the stack of blankets tighter. "I'd better, um, deliver these." Turning abruptly, she hurried away.

Zoe stared after her, slightly puzzled. No matter, it was time for lunch and she had promised to return a book that she'd borrowed from Vadivu.

Zoe scanned the cafeteria when she walked in, but it didn't surprise her to not see Chris. Whenever the E.R. got busy, the staff took their breaks on the fly.

Zoe grabbed a tray and got in line behind a trio of nurses whose whispered comments were punctuated with giggles. They reminded her of a high school clique. When one of them glanced around, her eyes widened.

"Hi, Dr. Hart!" she exclaimed with a friendly smile.

Feeling guilty for her thoughts, Zoe chatted with the nurses briefly as she selected a salad. After she had paid the cashier, she headed for her regular table.

When she did run into Chris, it would be hard to act as though nothing had changed between them. She would have to take her cue from him and to trust his discretion, because the last thing she would want was to be the subject of gossip and speculation.

When she got to the residents' table, it was nearly full. Marty glanced up and saw her, clearing his throat loudly. Immediately the conversation died as though a switch had been thrown. Except for a couple of mumbled greetings, everyone at the table began eating as though this were their last meal.

Marty, however, gave her a thumbs-up gesture.

"Way to go, girl," he said as Zoe set down her tray and dragged over a chair from a nearby table.

"Shh!" Barb smothered a giggle as she elbowed him.

Marty snorted in response, still looking up at Zoe.

"What are you talking about?" she asked, mildly curious as she sat down. "What's so funny?"

He shoved a forkful of spaghetti into his mouth and rolled his eyes. "Oh, *nothing*."

Feeling like an intruder, Zoe managed a stiff smile as she handed Vadivu her book.

"They're just being juvenile," Vadivu said sharply. "Pay no attention to them."

Zoe picked up her fork and poked at her salad, wishing she could say something about her meeting with Dr. Chester. However, she wasn't willing to risk starting a rumor about Dr. Codwell's retirement. The hospital grapevine was always churning out rumors about who was getting fired or divorced, or pregnant or sleeping with—

Zoe froze, her fork dropping from her nerveless fingers. It clattered onto the table, but she managed to keep it from falling to the floor. Surely even a one-horse town like this was beyond being scandalized by the idea of two unattached adults...

Of course it wasn't, if one of the suspected couple was the very attractive, very available head of the E.R. and the other was sometimes referred to as an "ice queen."

Barb looked up past Zoe's shoulder with a big smile. "Well, hello, Dr. Taylor," she drawled, her voice dripping with honey. "How are you today?"

Zoe struggled to keep her feelings hidden. Seeing him again, she experienced the same awareness as before, only now it was a hundred times stronger. Her body seemed to vibrate with it and her cheeks flamed.

"Doctors," he replied breezily as he looked around the table. His gaze seemed to linger on hers for an extra moment. "I trust that I'll see some of you later down in the E.R.," he added. "Enjoy your lunches."

Zoe released the breath she'd been holding without knowing it and turned her attention back to the salad that had somehow lost its appeal. She had made a big mistake, she realized with an ache in her chest. Unless she wanted to jeopardize her future and become the subject of gossip here at the hospital, it was something that she couldn't allow to happen again.

Barb leaned across the table toward Zoe.

"So," Barb demanded, "are the rumors about you and Dr. Taylor true?"

* * *

"Dammit!" Chris growled under his breath, slamming the flat of his hand against the empty men's room wall. He had meant to head Zoe off before she went to lunch in order to warn her about the speculation that was flying around about the two of them. Unfortunately a prospector with a self-inflicted gunshot wound had delayed him in the E.R. By the time he had finished digging a slug from the man's leg, Zoe had already left the maternity wing.

Chris slapped the wall again with his hand. He would be better off using his head for a battering ram.

He didn't care what people said about him. His position here was secure enough to weather a little whispering about his personal life. It was Zoe who would bear the brunt of the snickers. The two of them might as well have taken out a full-page ad in the weekly paper, the Thunder Canyon *Nugget,* to advertise what they had done.

Chris was toying with the idea of punching the wall with his fist when the door opened and a security guard he didn't know walked into the rest room. He gave Chris a curious glance before going over to a urinal.

Chris figured it was a good time for him to leave. For the rest of the afternoon, the E.R. kept him busy with a steady stream of people needing attention, including eight puking kids with food poisoning from a local day care, an overweight hiker complaining of chest pain and a tourist with a ruptured appendix.

Once Chris thought he glimpsed the back of Zoe's head by the triage station. He wanted desperately to talk with her, but by the time he was able to break away from a consult, she was gone.

At the end of the shift he looked out the window, but her car was gone from its earlier spot. He thought about calling her cell phone, but what he needed was to see her, to touch her and to bury his face in her sweet-smelling hair.

Then they needed to talk.

Chris changed out of his scrubs in the locker room and headed for her apartment, making one quick stop on the way. There was no sign of her car and no answer when he knocked on her door. Impatience building, he went back to his Beemer to wait her out.

It was full dark when Zoe turned down her street, still fuming over the way Barb had blindsided her at lunch. She had asked if the rumor was true that Chris's truck had been parked in front of Zoe's apartment until the wee hours. If Zoe's innocent expression and her regretful denial sounded as phony as they felt to her while she cringed inside, she'd fooled no one.

After a few nods and shrugs, her lunch mates had dropped the subject—at least until Zoe had pushed aside her half-eaten salad. When she'd walked out of the cafeteria, the feeling of being stared at while her personal life was dissected by people she barely knew made her skin burn as though she had rolled naked in a patch of nettles.

On the front seat next to her now were a bag of groceries she hardly remembered buying, a scarf she would never wear and a pair of shoes with heels that could very possibly break her ankles. Perhaps she would send the scarf, with its image of the Rocky Mountains, to her mother.

It was a good thing Zoe had already come to a decision about Chris, because when she got to her apartment and parked her car, he was waiting for her—and he was holding a bunch of long-stemmed peach roses wrapped in green paper.

The sight of him in tight jeans and worn boots sent a sizzle of reaction through her that all the reasoning in the world couldn't have resisted.

"Hi," he said, his grin a little crooked. "How was your day?"

The flash of uncertainty that crossed his face nearly melted Zoe's heart. "Had its ups and downs," she replied, recalling Dr. Chester's comments.

"Yeah," he replied. "I heard, and I'm sorry as hell for my part in the downside." He held out the flowers. "I wanted you to have these."

Zoe couldn't very well refuse to take them. Before she did, she glanced around, half expecting to see a cluster of paparazzi with telephoto lenses trained on the two of them. Realizing how paranoid her thoughts had become, she accepted the roses with a smile. Their color ranged from deep orange to pale apricot, their ruffled petals just beginning to unfurl.

"Thank you," she said. "They're lovely."

"We should talk." His hands hung at his sides as though he, too, was concerned about prying eyes. "Would it be okay for me to come in for a minute?"

Zoe bit her lip, struggling with temptation. He was right—they couldn't very well carry on a conversation out here on the street. It was all the justification she needed to put aside her recent resolution.

"Okay. I need to put these in water and I've got a bag of groceries in the car."

She waited while he retrieved her packages. Neither of them spoke again until they were safely inside her apartment. Setting aside the flowers, she dealt with their jackets. Dressed in a thin black sweater that hugged his shoulders, he seemed to fill up the room.

After she shut the door to the tiny coat closet, he cupped her shoulders gently with his hands while he peered into her face. He must have seen what he was looking for in her expression, because he leaned down slowly, giving her plenty of time to pull away.

"I missed you more than I wanted to," he muttered.

Zoe's defenses crumbled when he gathered her in his arms and kissed her with surprising tenderness. As soon as she opened her mouth to him, he turned up the heat. When he finally released her, she was having trouble breathing and his cheekbones were stained with color.

"That's not why I came here," he said, scrubbing one hand over his face. "Well, not the only reason." His smile flashed and then disappeared. "As soon as I heard the buzz at work, I wanted to warn you, to make sure you were okay. But as usual the E.R. was slammed with patients. I didn't get a minute to breathe until lunch, and by then you'd already left Maternity. My afternoon just got crazier."

"I thought about you," she admitted.

His eyes darkened. "I've hardly thought of anything but you since I left here the last time."

She wasn't sure how to respond to such an open declaration, so different from the dating games she was used to.

"Have a seat while I deal with these." She carried the flowers to the sink and then unloaded the odd mix of groceries she had grabbed off the shelves. "Turn on some music if you like," she suggested.

While she got a vase from the cupboard—a tower of sparkling crystal that her mother had insisted she might need—and filled it with water, he looked through her CDs. In a moment, an old Sarah McLachlan song called "Sweet Surrender" began to play.

"Would you like coffee?" Zoe asked, swaying to the music as she arranged the long stems.

When he didn't immediately reply, she glanced over her shoulder to see him watching her. His thumbs were hooked into his wide leather belt and he had a bemused expression on his face.

"Coffee?" she repeated, her throat suddenly tight. Probably better not to know what he was thinking since she was having so much trouble keeping her own thoughts in line.

"I should have asked right away—have you eaten?" he asked. "Do you want to go and get something?"

Now was the time to give the speech about her career coming first and her intention to not get involved with anyone while she was here in Thunder Canyon.

She opened her mouth to say the words at the same time that he reached out his hand and traced a line down her cheek with his fingertip.

"You put the roses to shame." His voice was husky.

The words should have come across as unbearably cheesy, a pickup line worthy of a low-class singles' bar. Spoken by anyone else, her reaction might have been to double over with derisive laughter.

All Zoe could do now was swallow hard as she stared, knowing beyond a doubt that she was in big trouble.

She held on to the little bit of sanity she had left. "We could order in a pizza," she suggested helplessly. "I've got salad makings and there's soda in the fridge."

Chapter Ten

When Zoe suggested they order a pizza, Chris's muscular shoulders seemed to relax. "That would be great," he replied.

She wondered what he would have said if she'd asked him to leave her alone. Would he have complied with a flash of that trademark grin and let her go without a protest or would he have tried to change her mind?

"Why don't you call for the pizza while I make the salad," she suggested. "The directory's in the second drawer down."

He took out his cell phone. "That's okay. Pizza delivery is on my speed dial. What's your pleasure?"

Zoe was getting the lettuce out of the refrigerator.

"Excuse me?" As she leaned past the open door, possible replies danced through her head like an X-rated conga line of Chippendales studs. Despite the blast of cool air, her face grew warm.

Chris looked so rugged, so male and so damned appealing as he stood there that she wanted to run her hands over his lean muscles as she had the other night. The memory brought a wave of heat to her cheeks.

The direction of her thoughts must have shown on her face, because he stuck up his hands as though she had pulled a gun.

"Hey, sweetie," he said with a lecherous grin, his blue eyes sparkling, "I was asking about pizza toppings, but I'm game for whatever you've got in mind."

It was impossible for Zoe to be embarrassed by his teasing. "Stick to the game plan, stud," she drawled. "I knew what you meant." She yanked open the produce drawer and poked through the plastic bags, looking for salad makings.

"I'll eat anything with sun-dried tomatoes and Feta cheese," she continued. "Do you like pesto?"

In addition to the lettuce she'd just purchased, she found part of a bell pepper, a couple of limp green onions and two celery stalks. Shutting the door of the fridge, she glanced at him expectantly.

"I'm sort of a ham-and-pineapple man myself," he drawled as she got out a knife and a small cutting board. "But I'm open to experimentation."

They compromised on a combo called the "Gold Nugget" that was topped with ham, pineapple, olives and four cheeses. While they waited for its arrival, he set the table and she made the salad. Neither of them brought up the gossip. Instead Zoe described her visit with Anna while she rinsed the lettuce and he sliced a ripe tomato.

"She's actually going to leave the abusive boyfriend?" Chris exclaimed with the knife poised over the cutting board. "Wow, that's great. She really did a one-eighty. So what turned her around, do you have any idea?"

A fresh burst of emotion filled Zoe. "I think I did."

With a lump in her throat, she repeated what Anna had told her. Chris listened intently. When she was done, he laid down the knife and wiped his hands on the front of his jeans.

"Honey, I am so proud of you." His voice brimmed with sincerity and approval as he opened his arms.

Zoe was blinded by unexpected tears. For a moment she allowed herself to lean against him, listening to the solid bump of his heart as he hugged her close.

"It feels good to connect with a patient like her and to know you made a difference, doesn't it?" he asked with his lips against her hair.

"This connection feels pretty good, too," she mumbled.

Briefly his arms tightened, but then he let her go. "Back to the salad," he said gruffly. "Someone has to be dressed in order to pay for the pizza when it gets here."

Zoe wasn't sure how to respond, so she began tearing the lettuce in the colander.

"How was your dinner with Faith and Cam?" she asked. What she really wanted to know was whether Chris had invited her as a last-minute replacement for a date who had canceled. Or, when Zoe had turned him down, had he asked someone else? She doubted he had trouble finding dates.

"For me to tag along with a newly engaged couple as crazy about each other as those two is like putting nipples on a bull," he said drily.

Zoe blinked up at him. "I beg your pardon?" Did bulls even *have* nipples? She supposed they must.

"Totally unnecessary. I could have left before the food arrived and they wouldn't have noticed."

"That's too bad." She was pleased to hear that he hadn't taken someone else with him after all.

"Don't get me wrong," he added hastily. "I couldn't be happier that my sister has found a guy like Cam. I know they didn't mean to ignore me or anything like that. They were just too busy oogling and cuddling to pay much attention."

"Oogling?" Zoe echoed as she dumped the lettuce into a bowl and added the sliced tomato.

"Shall I demonstrate?" Chris offered.

She held up her hands to ward him off. "I get the picture and I'd rather you cut up the celery."

Looking disappointed, he complied. Working side by side with him in her kitchen made her feel pleasantly domesticated—as though they were a team.

"So not being the center of attention causes you to pout?" she teased when the salad was finished.

His brows shot up. "That's why I invited you, sweetheart, to keep me entertained while they pawed each other."

She was groping for a witty comeback when the doorbell rang. "That must be the pizza," she said, wiping her hands on a towel.

After she looked through the peephole, she opened the door to a boy wearing a red cap and a matching jacket. She took the savory-smelling box and Chris pulled out his wallet. She noticed that he added a generous tip.

"Thanks, Doc," the delivery boy said with a jaunty salute before he left.

"Does everyone in this town know who you are?" Zoe asked as she opened the box and inhaled the aroma, then transferred the pie to a serving plate.

"Pretty much. I can't get away with anything."

While she tossed the salad, he poured their soda.

"Why didn't you tell me that before you left your truck sitting outside my apartment for half the night?" she muttered, reaching around him for the dressing. "Where did you park this time?"

"I drove my car today," he said. "It's down the street."

Hands on her hips, Zoe studied him. "And that's because you figured a black Beemer with doctor's plates would blend in better than a pickup truck?" she asked. "This isn't Beverly Hills."

Back in a city that was obsessed with being known and being seen, there was still a blessed anonymity that a small town like Thunder Canyon would never have.

"Perhaps you'd like me to go out and throw a camouflage net over my car," he suggested wryly.

"I have nothing to hide, but thanks for offering," she retorted. Oh, hell, let people talk if they had nothing better to do!

He pulled out her chair. "I wasn't making assumptions when I parked down the street." There was a defensive edge to his tone. "I was just trying to be discreet, since it's obvious that someone must have driven by the other night and recognized my truck."

"It's always wise not to assume," she agreed mildly when he took his seat at the small table. "I hope you like light Italian dressing. It's all I have on hand."

"It's perfect," he replied. "This is great."

"You paid for the pizza and helped make the salad," she reminded him. Her father had never done anything around the house, but Zoe was always impressed by men who did.

"Sharing the chores cuts the time in half," Chris replied. "My dad always helped out when he was home, so I guess he set a good example. Mom didn't treat me any different from my sisters when it came to cooking and cleaning, so I grew up to be very self-sufficient."

He put a piece of pizza on her plate while she dished up his salad. "How about you?" he asked. "Were you raised with servants?"

"We had a housekeeper," Zoe admitted, "but she wasn't there all the time and my parents both worked a lot, so I had to fend for myself, too."

"Are you a good cook?" he asked.

"I get by," she replied. "How about you? Can you make anything besides that delicious spaghetti sauce?"

"That's Mom's recipe." He wiggled his brows expressively. "Come over sometime and find out."

Zoe ignored the flutter of awareness. "The pizza's getting cold," she observed.

By implied consent, they didn't discuss the rumors while they ate. They talked about his dog, Ringo, and her mother's Persian cat, Heloise. They compared the movies they had rented and swapped horror stories about med school.

Between bites, they discussed the growing workload at the hospital.

"The board has hired an agency to recruit more RNs," Chris said, helping himself to the last piece of pizza after Zoe shook her head. "The hospital director, Joe Bell, came from a small hospital in Oregon," he continued. "He's done a decent job, more or less, but he's tightfisted as hell and he has no vision. We could use two additional E.R. doctors and we desperately need another half dozen trauma nurses."

Zoe sipped her soda without comment. She had

heard similar grumbling among the staff upstairs in Maternity.

Chris was about to take a bite when his eyes widened. "Well, that was imprudent of me," he muttered. "Just forget that I said anything about Bell, okay?"

Zoe blotted her mouth and scooted back her chair. "As long as you never tell anyone that I passed out cold at my first autopsy," she replied, stacking their dishes. "I wouldn't be able to live it down if word got out."

Wearing a solemn expression, Chris traced an X on his chest. "Cross my heart, your secret's safe with me." He got to his feet and carried their utensils to the counter. "You do realize that we're bonded for life now, don't you?"

Flustered by the intensity of his expression, Zoe began loading the dishwasher without commenting. After a moment he closed the empty pizza box.

"Where's the Dumpster?" he asked, ignoring the sudden awkwardness that had sprung up between them. "I'll take out the garbage."

While he was gone, Zoe made fresh coffee. Then she ducked into the bathroom and stared at her reflection to make sure that nothing was stuck in her teeth.

The face looking back at her was full of confusion. Part of her wanted to pursue whatever might be growing between her and Chris while she ignored any possible consequences to either her heart or her career. The cautious little voice inside her head whispered a reminder that people who took foolish chances often got hurt.

When she heard the front door open and close, she went back out to the living room.

"Miss me?" he asked with a cocky grin.

She pressed her hand to her heart. "Of course," she said brightly, even though she was determined to be cautious. If you stayed in control of your feelings, you could walk away without regrets.

She poured their coffee and led the way to the living room, ignoring her sudden nervousness. Settling on the couch, she kicked off her shoes and tucked one foot beneath her other thigh.

"This is a nice place." Chris sat next to her, stretching his arm across the back of the couch. "I'll bet it's a lot quieter than hospital housing."

"It's not bad." Zoe blew on her coffee. "I like the privacy here."

Her comment caused him to frown as he set his mug on her coffee table.

"Once again I apologize for subjecting you to all the gossip." His face had turned serious. "I really wish I had remembered to move the truck, but I wasn't exactly using my brain at the time."

"You're really being too hard on yourself," she protested, dismayed by his obvious remorse. "People like to talk, and we both know that hospitals are like little towns in themselves."

He was still frowning, so she pressed on. "What

happened was no big deal." She waved her hand. "It was an impulse, that's all. We need to put it past us and move on. Tomorrow they'll be talking about something else."

"That's certainly one way of describing it," he said slowly. "No big deal."

Funny, but when he said the words, they made her feel awful. She held her breath, waiting to see if he would argue.

He reached for his coffee without saying anything more and took a long swallow. To her surprise, he got to his feet and carried his half-full mug over to the kitchen counter. When he turned, he was smiling, so she knew he wasn't upset. He was probably relieved that she wasn't overreacting.

"I'm sorry to eat and run," he said, shoving his hands into his pockets. "I'm glad we talked and I appreciate the meal, but I just remembered that the guy who comes by to feed the animals had to go to Butte this afternoon for a dental appointment." He shrugged. "I need to get home and do the chores before the stock mutinies on me."

She wasn't too sure just what horses did when they mutinied, but she wasn't about to argue. Hiding her disappointment, she got up from the couch.

"I understand," she said. She got his jacket from the closet and held it out. "Thanks again for the roses. They remind me of California sunsets."

He glanced at the bouquet on her side table as he shrugged into the jacket. "That's what I was aiming for, all right."

With his hand on the doorknob, he hesitated. His gaze roamed her face. "There's a nice steak place in town called Sebastian's. Have you been there?"

"I haven't been much of anywhere," she replied on a surge of renewed hope.

"Do you want to have dinner after work tomorrow?" he asked.

Zoe came to a sudden decision. If he still wanted to see her, even knowing the eventual outcome, she was going to indulge herself. "I'd like that."

After they settled on a time for him to pick her up, he tipped up her chin and leaned closer. Briefly his fingers increased their pressure as he covered her mouth in a hot, hard kiss. She felt the sizzling contact right down to her toes, but before she could respond, he released her.

His eyes blazed into hers. "See you tomorrow." Without waiting for her response, he opened the door and left.

Wrapping her arms around her quivering middle, Zoe watched his departing figure until he turned up the street and disappeared into the night. Not once did he look back.

When Chris reached his car and slid behind the wheel, he could still feel the touch of her lips against his mouth. Leaving her tonight had been damned difficult, but he didn't figure the sense of loss was anything compared to the wrenching separation he was going to feel when the time came to let her go. Her future plans might be set in concrete, but his were suddenly filled with questions whose answers he was determined to explore.

"Are you seeing Dr. Taylor again?" Vadivu asked when she walked into the locker room a few days later.

Zoe had changed into jeans and a thick sweater for her visit to his ranch. "Afraid so," she replied as she pulled on her boots.

When she got to her feet, she smiled at the other woman's reflection in the mirror. "We're stopping for burgers and then we're going to his place so I can help with the animals." She wrinkled her nose. "That should be fun."

Over dinner at Sebastian's the other night, Chris had suggested to her that they end the speculation at work by having lunch together in the cafeteria the next day. According to the grapevine, they were now a couple.

Vadivu worked lotion into her hands. "Have you thought about what you'll do when your residency is up?" she asked. "Might you stay on here?"

Her question raised issues that Zoe had been doing her best to ignore. "Hey, slow down," she said with an artificial laugh as she applied fresh gloss to her lips. "I've only been seeing Chris for a short time. We aren't serious."

Although he had kissed her passionately on several occasions, he had made no attempt to sleep with her again. Zoe wasn't sure whether to be relieved or annoyed by his restraint. Mostly she was just plain frustrated.

"It may not be serious yet," Vadivu warned as she ran a brush through her heavy black hair, "but I've seen the way he looks at you in the E.R. It's very romantic."

Zoe shook her head as though doing so could ward off Vu's words. Zoe wasn't about to discuss the amazing physical compatibility she had with Chris. "We're just having fun, but we both know it can't go anywhere," she said instead.

Vadivu rolled her dark eyes. "Tell Dr. Taylor that, not me." She had begun hanging out with a lab tech from Bombay and she'd confided in Zoe that both of their families approved.

"You've got romance on the brain because of John," Zoe retorted.

Giggling softly, Vadivu sprayed perfume on the honey-tanned skin of her throat. "At least *we* haven't made it to the hospital grapevine top-ten list like some people in this room." She sighed dramatically. "I have to tell you, though, that you're old news since last night's slugfest in the parking lot between the ICU nurse and her husband."

"I heard he'd been drinking," Zoe replied as she twisted her hair into a knot on top of her head, letting the shorter strands hang loose. "I feel bad for her."

"So do I." Vu dug through her oversize purse until she found her cell phone. "Have a good time cleaning stalls."

"You, too." Zoe made a face before she left. As she drove to old town to meet Chris a few moments later, she rehashed the other resident's comments. If Chris was falling for Zoe as Vadivu claimed, why did he seem content with a kiss at the door?

Her father had called on her cell phone this afternoon, returning the message she'd left him three days ago. He made no effort to remember her schedule even though she e-mailed it every week, so it was sheer luck that he'd caught her on a break. As usual, he had asked how she was and then barreled ahead without giving her a chance to respond before handing her off to his wife. Frustrated, Zoe ended up trying to explain to Marcus that she had to go back to work.

"I'm worried about Juliet," Chris said as he drove Zoe out to his place after they left The Hitching Post. Talking about the pregnant waitress beat trying to analyze Zoe.

She had been unusually quiet during dinner, making him think she might beg off going home with him, but she hadn't. "I don't think she's taking good care of herself," he added.

"I know. The poor girl looks tired." Zoe rested her hand on the console between them. When he gave it a squeeze, she linked her fingers with his. How pathetic he had gotten that such a simple gesture would make his nerves tingle with anticipation.

For the last week he had reined in his desire to make

love to her again in order to show her that he wanted more from her than sex. A couple of times when he had forced himself to let her go, he'd thought he'd glimpsed a reflection of his own frustration on her face.

He didn't know how much longer he could resist temptation, not when the memory of losing himself in her woke him up at night bathed in sweat and hard as a railroad spike.

"Do you know whether Juliet is planning to stop working soon?" Zoe asked as his house came in sight. "Being on her feet so much can't be good for her."

"She seemed to appreciate your interest," Chris replied. "If I were pregnant, I think I'd prefer a female doctor."

"Honey, if you were pregnant, you'd have your choice of any doctor you wanted," Zoe chuckled. "Sorry, but I couldn't resist."

Chris tightened his grip on her hand. "I should have seen that coming."

"Seriously, I promise to save my lecture on the need for more women's health care until another time," Zoe added.

It was an opening he couldn't ignore. "Then I'll save my comment about the town's need for another OB/GYN until then, as well."

Her silence didn't surprise him. Perhaps it was too soon to mention the future, but he was falling hard. Already the thought of losing her scared the hell out of him.

Releasing her hand, he turned into his driveway.

"Well, here comes the welcoming committee," he said when he saw Ringo.

What had Chris expected Zoe to say—that some guy she'd started sleeping with was suddenly more important than the career she'd worked so hard to accomplish? How would he feel if the situation was reversed?

As soon as Zoe opened her door, the dog ran around to her side of the car as though Chris had ceased to exist. He hoped that Ringo would remember his manners and not jump up on her.

"Hey, boy." Zoe extended her hand. "Remember me?"

The dog promptly sat on his butt in the driveway and extended his paw, ears pricked and tongue lolling. Where the hell had he learned that?

Not from Chris, who was tempted to follow Ringo's example.

Chris tried to picture the small ranch through Zoe's eyes as she looked around. This place had been home for as long as he could remember. There was nowhere he would rather live.

In the glow from the porch light, did the house hold any charm for someone like Zoe? Did the stable and the corral fences look run-down in the cold glow from the utility pole? Did the smell overwhelm her?

He took her hand, wishing she would speak.

"Before we visit the animals, could I use your bathroom?" she asked.

* * *

As Zoe followed Chris up the front steps, she could imagine sitting on the wide porch in a pair of matching rocking chairs as the evenings grew milder and the chores were done. Something tugged at her when she thought of how relaxing it would be to discuss the events of the day as they rocked in unison, admiring the view.

After Chris unlocked the front door, he reached inside to switch on a light.

"Welcome," he said, stepping back to let her go in first.

"I thought you country types didn't believe in locking your doors," she said, unzipping her jacket.

"Never used to," he replied as he slipped it from her shoulders, "but one of the neighbors had a break-in a couple of months ago. Even with Ringo on guard, locking the doors seemed like a good idea after that."

The dog, who had followed them inside, cocked his head at the sound of his name.

"I'd almost forgotten what a pretty place this is," Zoe commented as she stood in the entry and looked around.

"Powder room's still down the hall," Chris told her. "I'll feed the pooch and get some coffee started unless you'd rather have tea."

Zoe rested her hand on the bathroom door frame, which had been refinished to a satin sheen. "Coffee's fine, thanks." No one got through medical school and internship without developing a fondness for caffeine.

When she came back out, the furnace was humming as it took off the chill and she could hear Chris in the kitchen. Without being straight-out nosy, she took the opportunity to look around again on her way back through the house.

Although it was definitely old-fashioned with its high ceilings and the rock fireplace in the living room, its appeal was growing on her.

As she ran her hand over the dark wood banister, he appeared in the doorway wearing a concerned expression.

"What is it?" she asked, hoping he hadn't been called back to work while she'd been in the powder room. "Is something wrong?"

He crossed the room and took her face in his hands. "Yes, something is very wrong." His voice was deeper than normal as he brushed one thumb across her lower lip. "I haven't kissed you in way too long," he whispered.

The warmth of his fingers on her sensitive skin and the intensity of his gaze sent reaction flooding through her. She gripped his wrists to keep from sinking to the floor in a boneless heap.

"Zoe, I'm crazy about you," he said right before his mouth covered hers. "Stay with me tonight, please."

Chapter Eleven

Zoe could hardly pull away in the middle of a kiss—a very hot, openmouthed kiss—to ask whether he was talking about her spending the night with him now or staying on in Thunder Canyon. When he wrapped his arms around her and held her close, she forgot to think at all.

By the time he finally let her go, she was in no condition to formulate a coherent question. Her heart was hammering like the drum in a marching band and she nearly forgot to breathe.

Face flushed, Chris managed a devilish grin as he tucked a strand of Zoe's hair behind her ear with his finger. His other arm was still curved around her, his hand splayed on her hip to anchor her against him.

"Ready to help me clean stalls?" he asked.

Zoe blinked up at him as he let her go and reality sank in. "I think some fresh air will do us both some good," she agreed. Lifting her arms, she made sure the clip in her hair was secure.

"Lead on, MacFarmer."

"That's MacRancher to you," he retorted as he grabbed her hand. "The coffee should be ready. Let's take a couple of mugs with us."

While her body still simmered from the heat of their embrace, he apparently had no trouble switching from passionate lover to joking companion. One thing was for sure, her opportunity to ask exactly what he had meant earlier was now gone.

Minutes later they carried their coffee through the cool evening to the stable. In the corral a group of horses crowded eagerly against the fence. Ears twitching, feet stamping, they nickered an impatient welcome.

"They're beautiful," Zoe exclaimed.

"Come on," Chris urged when she would have lingered to visit. "Let's get the stalls ready. You can make friends after I let them inside."

He showed her how to measure out the grain and fill the hay nets while he shoveled up the soiled bedding from each stall. Although they bantered and teased each other while they worked, Zoe could feel the awareness building between them. Sneaking glances, imagining him all hot and sweaty, made her want to strip off his clothes right in the stable and run her hands all over him.

When he caught her watching him, his smile disappeared. He set down the wheelbarrow and stalked toward her, never taking his gaze from her face.

Zoe began to tremble and her mouth went dry. Her feet had lost the will to move. When he reached her, he grabbed her hips and hauled her up against him without saying a word. As he lifted her, she clung to his neck, wrapping her legs around his waist and straining against him through two layers of denim. She kissed the warm salty skin of his throat while he carried her through an open doorway into a small room and set her on the edge of some sort of low cabinet.

He kissed her, his tongue sliding against hers. She yanked open the snaps of his shirt and pulled it free from his jeans. When her hands reached his bare skin, sliding up his torso, he groaned.

His breathing was harsh as he shrugged out of his jacket and unzipped her parka. When she lifted her arms, he peeled her sweater over her head and fumbled with the front clasp of her bra. Frantic to feel his hands on her, she freed it for him and leaned back on her arms.

He covered her breasts with his hands and stroked her sensitized nipples with his thumbs. When she gasped her pleasure, he bent his head. After a moment she cradled his jaw in her hands and fused her mouth to his while she reached for the buckle of his belt.

He pulled away with a groan. In a few deft movements, he yanked off her boots and stripped her from the waist down. Tossing a folded blanket onto the cabinet, he set her back down and kissed her again. Amid their mingled gasps and sighs, she unzipped his fly and freed him. As she pushed down his jeans and shorts, she realized vaguely that his Broncos cap was still on his head.

He caressed her intimately with his long clever fingers, making her forget all about the damned cap. Burning with need, she slid to the edge of the cabinet and spread her legs wide, offering herself. He braced one arm against the wall behind her as she guided him into her. For a moment he held himself still. Hands on his hips, she pressed against him, sobbing when he started to move.

He felt so good that she thought she would come apart. As he drove into her, she shattered around him, muffling her cries against his shoulder as the spasms shook her. His body went rigid and then he began to shudder as she held on tight.

When he collapsed against her, neither of them moved as they both struggled for breath.

"Are you okay?" he asked eventually, untangling himself.

"Mmm," was all she could manage. Her entire body was limp, as though her bones had dissolved and all her circuits had melted. She shifted herself around on the blanket with her legs discreetly closed. "Oh, yeah," she finally added as she recovered. "Okay is definitely an understatement."

He had pulled up his jeans and tucked in his shirttail. He bent down and picked up her clothes.

After he had put his jacket back on and she'd turned her jeans right side out, he laid his hand against her cheek.

"The shower back at the house is big enough for two," he said, buckling his belt. "I'll let you put yourself back together while I bring in the horses. I'm surprised they haven't knocked down the fence."

A little while later, Chris stood in the doorway to the living room and studied Zoe as she sat curled in front of the fire wearing his maroon velour robe. They had made love a second time in the shower and then again on his king-size bed.

The pan of frozen lasagna he'd stuck into the oven earlier was nearly ready. He wasn't sure about her, but he'd managed to work up a considerable appetite.

Something must have alerted her to his presence in the doorway, because she looked up at him and smiled. The deep V of the robe framed the shadowy cleavage between her breasts. Briefly he considered turning down the oven so the lasagna wouldn't burn while he took her back to bed, but his stomach chose that moment to growl loudly.

"Dinner's nearly ready," he said. "How about some wine while I warm the bread?"

"Wine sounds lovely." She tightened the belt of his

robe when she got to her feet. "If you're going to indulge, don't forget that I'll need a lift back to my car."

"Why don't you stay over?" he suggested. "I've got
to go in early tomorrow, so I can drop you at your car
on my way."

Her smile faltered. "I can't stay. Tomorrow's my
day off. I was planning to sleep in and then I've got a
list of chores." She rested her hands lightly on his chest,
her eyes full of secrets. "I'm sorry. Do you mind?"

"When you look at me like that, how can I resist?" He kept his tone light while he smoothed her
lapel. "The robe looks better on you than it ever did
on me."

"Even so," she replied, "I think I'll get dressed, if I
have time."

He waved her away. "Go ahead." It was plain to see that
she was intent on establishing boundaries and regaining
a sense of control. "Anything to get out of setting the
table, I suppose," he added as he went back to the kitchen.

When she joined him, he saw that she had pinned her
hair back up and put on lipstick. In her simple white
sweater and snug jeans, she took his breath away.

He handed her a glass of wine. "You're the best-
looking stable hand I've seen in a long time," he murmured, saluting her with the other glass. Since he'd be
driving, it held about an inch of ruby liquid.

"That's the nicest toast that I've ever heard," she replied after they'd each taken a sip, "and the lasagna
smells wonderful. Suddenly I'm starving."

"I thought we'd eat in here," he replied. "It's cozier." He had lit a fat candle in the center of the small round table to go with the trio burning on the granite counter.

"You've made this entire house wonderfully warm and cozy," she replied as he put the hot pan on a trivet and set out the basket of bread. "Have you redone every room yourself?"

"Pretty much. I've still got some painting to finish and I didn't do all of the remodeling." After he held out her chair, he sat facing her and unfolded his napkin. "I bartered for the plumbing," he explained as they helped themselves to the food.

She sprinkled grated cheese on her lasagna. "You set a sink and I'll set your broken bone?" she asked.

"He needed a horse trained for his daughter so she could start barrel racing," Chris replied with a chuckle. "As it turned out, I ended up setting her broken arm, too. I think he installed the ice maker for that."

"Ouch." Zoe puckered her lips into a pout that made him want to lean over and taste them. They looked slightly swollen, making him wonder if she was tender in other places, too.

Abruptly he covered her hand as it rested on the table. "I want you to know that what we have together isn't just physical for me." He stroked her smoothed skin with his thumb. Every inch of her was like satin, her scent far sweeter than a meadow filled with wildflowers. "It's a lot more than that."

She dropped her gaze to their hands. "Me, too," she said, but she didn't sound very happy about it.

When Chris dropped Zoe off at her car an hour later, she knew he was disappointed that she hadn't responded with more enthusiasm to his earlier comment. Conversation had grown a little stilted after that. She had offered to help him clean up the dishes, but he'd seemed in a hurry to get rid of her.

"Are you okay?" she asked him now, after he had walked her to her car and held open the door. The street wasn't busy. Under the glow from the streetlights, there was no one else around.

He grasped her elbows. "Don't worry. I'll be fine." He gave her a brief kiss. "Do you want me to follow you, just to make sure you get home safely?"

"Thanks, but it's not necessary." It would be so easy to get used to this, she realized, and to become dependent on him. The passion that flared between them was like a drug that made her powerless. When he smiled and she felt her control slipping away, she struggled to regain it.

"I think we need to slow things down," she blurted.

Shock flared across his face, but then he swallowed and dredged up a smile. "If that's what you want," he conceded, "then of course that's what we'll do."

His words filled her with relief at his willingness to let her set the pace. "Thank you," she said, patting his cheek. "I'll talk to you soon."

* * *

Later that night, she dreamed that she was sitting in a small rowboat, drifting away from shore on a dark, foggy night. She wanted to go back, but the oars were missing. When she tried to paddle with her hands, she realized she was chained to the empty oarlock.

As the tide carried her farther from shore, the mists parted and she saw a group of people standing on a dock watching her. Among them was her mother, wearing one of her expensive business suits. She was deep in conversation with a well-dressed older couple.

"Mom!" Zoe cried. "Help me!"

Patrice looked around and saw Zoe. She held up her briefcase. "I've got a meeting, dear," she called. "You can manage on your own." She and the couple disappeared through the crowd.

As the boat bobbed farther from shore, Zoe recognized her father standing near the edge of the dock with Marcus on his shoulder.

"Daddy!" Zoe cried, pulling on her chains more urgently. "I'm out here!"

Her father pointed her out to Marcus and then they both waved.

"Let's go, Daddy," Marcus said. "I'm hungry."

"What about me?" Zoe shouted as they turned away. The boat was drifting faster now, the waves higher as they carried her farther out to sea. Even if she managed to free herself, she wasn't sure she would be able to swim to shore on her own.

Suddenly she spotted a blond head in the crowd. Hope flared anew.

"Chris!" she shouted, rattling the chains frantically. "I can't get loose and I've lost the oars."

When he looked out over the water and saw her, she went limp with relief. For the first time, she noticed another boat tied up to the dock.

"Do something!" she screamed as the waves grew stronger and her boat rocked wildly. "Don't let me go!"

He stood with his hands in his pockets as the fog thickened. "I'm doing what you asked," he called back to her. "I'm giving you space." He watched her, hands in his pockets, as the fog thickened.

In moments, the dock would disappear from sight. "Chris!" she pleaded more urgently. "Fight for me!"

Zoe woke up shivering under the blankets in a bed that felt as though it had been tossed helplessly about in a dark, menacing sea. She rolled over and reached out, hands free, but the bed was empty and she was alone.

Chris invited her to go with him to a small rodeo in a neighboring town on Saturday to watch him compete in the calf-roping event.

"It will be Denver's first time out," he added, leaning on the counter at one end of the admissions desk where Zoe was catching up on paperwork. "I'm eager to see how he performs in front of the crowd."

Zoe glanced at the receptionist seated at the other

end of the counter, but she was busy talking on the phone while she worked on the computer.

"I'd love to go, but I think I've got other plans," Zoe replied, torn between temptation and hesitation.

His expression didn't falter when he straightened away from the counter. "Sure, I understand. We'll do it another time, then," he said with his usual easy smile.

The receptionist hung up the phone. "Hello, Dr. Taylor," she said. "Do you need anything?"

"No, thanks. I'm good," he replied. "Well, I'd better get back to the E.R.," he told Zoe. "See you later."

Frustrated, she watched him saunter back through the double doors. He was letting her slip away without a struggle, she told herself, as though hanging on to what they had found with each other wasn't worth the effort.

A few moments later when one of the nurses approached the counter, Zoe's feelings were still a swirl of confusion.

"My son's baseball league is having an equipment swap Saturday morning," the nurse said. "I'm looking for volunteers to help out, if you're interested."

"Why not." Zoe didn't give herself time to reconsider. It wasn't as though she had anything better to do this weekend.

When she walked into the gym on Saturday morning wearing jeans and an old college sweatshirt, the smell immediately reminded her of high school basketball games and PE class. PE had been her least favorite subject.

A woman sat at a table inside the door. Behind her was a sign that said *Table Rental $10*.

"I'm just here to help," Zoe explained.

"We need all the help we can get," she replied. "Go on in."

A couple of men were setting up more tables around the perimeter of the gym while other people unloaded boxes of gear. A group of children played a noisy game of tag, darting around stacks of folding chairs, and a country song pumped out of a portable CD player on one of the tables.

"Hey, Doc Hart!" Nancy, the nurse who had asked her to come, introduced her to a heavyset woman in a faded red sweat suit.

"Maureen is in charge," Nancy said. "This is Dr. Hart."

"Please call me Zoe," she corrected. "What can I do to help?"

Maureen consulted her clipboard, then looked around. "Why don't the two of you set up some chairs," she suggested. "Leave plenty of room for people to walk between the two rows of tables."

"Thanks for coming," Nancy said as she walked with Zoe to the pile of folded chairs. "The money we'll make today will go into the league treasury."

Zoe thought of Chris, wondering what time his calf-roping event started. She would have enjoyed watching him compete, but it was her own dumb fault that she was here unfolding chairs instead.

She noticed a display holding aluminum bats and a rack of batting helmets. "Don't the teams furnish all this stuff?" she asked Nancy as they walked past the equipment.

"Some of it, of course, bats and balls. Batting helmets." Nancy carried a chair under each arm and Zoe did the same. "Kids need mitts and cleats," Nancy continued. "They all outgrow shoes and not every parent can buy new ones each season, so they recycle the old ones. Today will be more buy and sell than actual swapping."

She looked around her with hands on her ample hips. "That's enough chairs for now. I need to run to the ladies' room before the sale starts and then my son's team is selling homemade cookies. Why don't you check back with Maureen."

When the work was done, Zoe ended up watching two little girls for a former patient who wanted to sell her older daughter's outgrown equipment.

After Zoe bought the girls each a cookie from Nancy's booth, she was walking them back to their mom when a boy barreled into her.

He looked up, red hair poking around the edges of his cap, and she recognized him instantly.

"Sorry, Dr. Hart!" Erik exclaimed, his freckled face glowing with excitement.

She gave his thin shoulder a reassuring pat. "No problem, Sport. Are you here with your dad?"

"Uh-uh," he replied. "Dad had a meeting."

"I brought him."

She looked up, straight into Chris's deep blue eyes. He, too, wore a baseball cap.

Guilt rushed through her, even though she had nothing to feel guilty about.

"What are you doing here?" she demanded. "I thought you'd be at the rodeo."

His eyebrows rose in response to her tone. "Like my man here said, Cam had a meeting and I got recruited. Faith got called out at the last minute and this swap is too good to miss." He glanced down at the boy beside him. "Right, Erik?"

"That's right, Doc—Uncle Chris," Erik replied, his gaze darting to Zoe. "He was going to ride his horse, but he said he'd *much* rather come here!"

Chris gave Zoe a warning glance, as though she might say the wrong thing and hurt the boy's feelings. "Anytime, Buddy," Chris replied. "Just think of me as a pinch hitter."

"I need a mitt," Erik announced. "Can we go and look before they're all gone?"

"Check out what they've got at that table," Chris replied. "I'm right behind you, so wait for me."

Zoe watched Erik dart around a woman pushing a stroller, his bright green jacket making him easy to track.

Shifting to block Zoe's path, Chris nudged her out of the aisle. "I didn't expect to see you here," he said.

"They needed volunteers," she replied. "Nancy Baumgartner asked me if I'd mind. Her son plays T-ball."

He studied her face. "I didn't know that you and Nancy were tight."

"We work together," she replied shortly, as though that explained everything. "There's a lot you don't know about me."

He nodded as though he was conceding a point.

"I'm surprised Cam isn't buying new gear for Erik," she commented, "especially when Faith works in a sporting-goods store."

"He wanted to, but Erik's heart is set on a mitt that's already broken in, so here we are," Chris explained.

"Uncle Chris!" Erik appeared at his arm, tugging at his sleeve. "I found a perfect mitt. The lady is holding it, but you gotta come quick!"

"You heard him," Chris told Zoe. "I gotta go *quick,* so I'll see you later."

She was about to turn away and make her escape when she noticed her patient waving wildly from the table next to the one where Erik was waiting for Chris. Reluctantly Zoe followed him through the crowd.

"Can you watch my stuff for a minute?" the other woman asked as soon as Zoe got within hearing distance. She held up a cell phone. "My husband is calling from Seattle, and it's too loud in here."

"Sure," Zoe said. "Go ahead."

After the woman hurried away with her daughters in tow, Zoe sat down next to the bats and three pairs of girls' cleats that looked pretty worn. She was watching the people walk by when she heard Erik's voice over the buzz of conversation.

"I asked her first!" He sounded upset.

When Zoe stood up, she could see that he and another boy had hold of the same mitt.

"I want this one!" the boy told his dad, who stood next to Chris. "It's Tommy Herbert's old glove."

Chris reached for the mitt, attempting to extricate it from the boys. "Sorry, son," he said. "My nephew's right. He saw it first."

The other boy tried to yank it away. "No!" he cried. "You can't have it."

A circle opened up around the table as other people stopped to watch the exchange, but Zoe had a clear view from her chair. The other man stood half a head shorter than Chris. In the sea of T-shirts and jeans, he was dressed in an elegant designer suit. When he turned, she glimpsed his hawklike profile above the knot of his tie that was similar to the ones her father wore, probably Italian silk.

"You heard him, kid," he told Erik in a deep, booming voice as he took out his wallet. "You need to find a different mitt." He looked at the woman behind the table, whose cheeks were flushed crimson with embarrassment. "How much?" he demanded.

Haltingly she named a figure that sounded reasonable to Zoe.

Chris was still hanging on to the mitt while Erik's

lip jutted out and he looked ready to cry. "We're buy-ing it," Chris said firmly as he held out some bills to the woman.

Erik's lip retreated and he grinned up at Chris.

"I'll double it," the other man said.

The woman's hand froze in midair without taking Chris's money, as her gaze darted back and forth. "My son was the league MVP for three years running," she said proudly. "The mitt's a Wilson that I probably priced way too low."

Chris leaned down and said something to Erik that was drowned out by the other boy's whine. When Chris straightened again, Zoe expected to see his accommo-dating smile as he let the other boy win but instead, his expression remained firm.

"Did you agree to hold the glove for my nephew?" he asked the woman.

Her head bobbed. "Yeah, but—"

"To be fair, I'll give you what this gentleman of-fered," he continued, cutting her off. "That's all I'm pre-pared to pay."

The other boy's face turned red and his wail grew louder. "I want it, I want it, I want it!" he chanted.

"You heard him," the suit exclaimed, his voice ris-ing as he took out more bills and waved them in front of the seller's face. "I'll double the price again."

Her eyes widened and she licked her lips. The peo-ple who had been murmuring to each other behind their hands suddenly fell silent.

"Put your money away," Chris said quietly. "It's already sold."

Zoe couldn't see his expression, but when he held out the money the woman snatched it before taking a step backward. Zoe doubted that she was looking at Chris's easygoing grin after all.

With a firm tug, he pulled the mitt away from the other boy and handed it to Erik, who wrapped his arms around the worn leather as though he were holding a brand-new puppy.

"Thank you!" he crowed, wearing a huge grin. "It's a winner. I can feel it!"

"Okay, friend, I know your game," the other man snarled, looking over his shoulder at the fascinated spectators as his boy tugged on his expensive suit jacket and blubbered out his disappointment. "I've got a plane to catch, so just tell me how much you want for the damn thing."

Finally Chris's smile blossomed. He touched his fingers to the brim of his hat in a mocking gesture as he urged Erik away from the table. "Sorry, *friend*. It's not for sale."

The man glared. "It will take more than a mitt to make that little runt into a decent player."

Chris stiffened and leaned down until the two men were nose to nose. Zoe hoped he never turned that icy expression on her.

"My nephew's not a runt," he said in a voice that could have cut glass, "but you're acting like a jerk in front of your boy. I think you should probably go catch your flight."

Zoe felt a rush of pride as she stared at Chris's determined profile. His quiet strength was evident in every line of his body as he faced down the other man. It was all she could do to keep from running over and throwing her arms around Chris's neck.

It wasn't merely pride flowing through her, she realized. It was love.

All her fears had come true.

"Yeah!" came a shout from the back of the crowd. "You tell him, Doc." A couple of other murmurs rose up, too.

Finally Maureen pushed her way through to the table and turned to face them with the clipboard still pressed to her ample chest.

"This has gone on long enough," she announced in a clear voice. "This transaction is final."

She turned her gaze on the man in the suit. "You, sir, are setting a poor example to our young athletes. You need to leave and the rest of you might as well move on. The sale's over in a half hour."

While Zoe continued to watch, Chris glanced down at Erik, whose smile had morphed into a worried frown. "Do you need shoes?" Chris asked.

Still clutching the mitt, Erik shook his head. "My new mom's using her discount at Extension Sports," he said clearly.

His comment brought on a few chuckles as people

moved on. Maureen tried to apologize to Chris, but he brushed her words aside. "Don't worry about it."

The woman whose table Zoe had been minding reappeared with her kids. "Thanks so much," she said. "I guess I missed the entertainment, but my husband's been gone for nearly a week on business and I've been dying to talk to him."

"No problem," Zoe replied, forcing a smile to lips that felt numb.

"That guy in the suit's a real jerk," the woman added. "Lucky for the rest of us that he travels a lot, so he's hardly ever at the games."

Zoe nodded numbly. By the time she managed to break away, Chris appeared to be deep in conversation with a couple of the other men. Emotions in a turmoil, Zoe managed to slip out the door.

Chapter Twelve

Chris had no idea what he was going to say to Zoe when he got to her apartment. He just knew that he had to see her.

Luckily Cam had called his cell as Chris and Erik were leaving the swap meet. Chris was able to drop Erik off at the diner to meet his dad and fend off Cam's gratitude for stepping in. After Chris assured him that he hadn't minded missing the rodeo, he'd used the necessity of taking care of his horse as an excuse not to stay for a burger.

When he got to Zoe's apartment, she opened the door as though she was expecting him. As always, her beauty hit him full force, even though she didn't appear pleased to see him.

"Did I come at a bad time?" he asked, suddenly re-alizing that she might have left the sale without saying goodbye because she had other plans.

"Not really." She opened the door wider. "Come on in."

After Chris's confrontation with Mitt-man, as he thought of the guy at the swap meet, adrenaline still pumped through his system like a drug. His arms ached to throw Zoe over his shoulder and carry her to the bedroom even though she had told him she wanted to slow things down.

He settled for a more conservative approach, reach-ing out and taking her hand. Her fingers were cold to the touch, but she didn't pull back.

"Honey, I missed you," he blurted, filled with the sudden overwhelming desire to lay his cards out on the table. "I'm not sure what's been going on lately with us—" He swallowed hard and forged ahead. "Taking it slow isn't working for me."

Her eyes widened and the shadows seemed to fade as her lips parted. The flush to her cheeks gave him the courage to continue.

"Zoe, I can't help my feelings." He was unable to stem the flow of words as he wrapped his hands around her slim wrists. "I'm falling for you."

When he was done speaking he felt an enormous rush of relief. Giving her time to absorb what he'd said, he lifted her hand and pressed a kiss to the inside of her wrist where the pulse throbbed.

The world stopped for him as she drew in a breath. Afraid to move, he waited for her reaction. "Say something," he pleaded as the silence between them spun out like line from a fishing reel. "Tell me that I'm not alone in this, that you feel something for me, too."

A frown formed a tiny pleat between her brows and her eyes darkened. His heart went into free fall as she disentangled her hands from his loose grip. He wanted to press his fingers to her lips to prevent the words he already knew with a sharp, piercing pain to his chest that he wouldn't want to hear.

"I'm sorry," she whispered, shaking her head. Her face had gone pale. "Nothing's changed and I'm not staying when my residency is over."

Not even for you. The unspoken words resounded in his head with a deafening cacophony of sound.

The excitement, the determination, the adrenaline that had been driving Chris so urgently leaked away, leaving him feeling weak and shaken. And unbearably, blindingly stupid. What had he been thinking to rush over here and push her like this after she had asked him to take it slow?

"Forget what I said." He kept his smile steady by sheer force of will. "No reason we can't keep it light and have some fun."

She began shaking her head while he was still talking. "It wouldn't be a good idea. Not now."

Not after he'd blown it by shoving his feelings in her face like a cream pie on a tacky comedy show.

"Why not?" he asked anyway, cupping her cheek with his hand.

She turned her face away from his touch, her eyes downcast. "I don't want…either of us to get hurt," she whispered.

Her hesitation barely registered as he took her hand again and pressed it against his chest. "I'll hurt if I can't keep seeing you," he said roughly. "We're good together. We can keep on…enjoying each other's company," he finished, picking his words carefully so he wouldn't sound crass.

She enjoyed making love with him, he knew that as surely as he knew how to fix a dislocated shoulder. This time she merely shook her head without speaking, but regret was plain to see in her expression.

"I understand," he said without understanding anything. He cleared his throat, but the lump stayed lodged there like a tumor. "Don't worry about work," he continued clumsily. "I won't, um, embarrass you or anything."

Her smile was sad. "I know that."

Finally he realized there was nothing left to say. This was all his fault for charging over here like an idiot on speed.

He moved one hand in a meaningless gesture, part surrender and part goodbye wave. When he reached for the knob and wrenched open her door, she didn't attempt to stop him. Gritting his teeth against the fresh flood of disappointment, he walked away.

* * *

Zoe was still seated on the couch with an afghan pulled over her, staring unseeingly through the front window at the wall of a nearby building as daylight turned to dusk. She had lost track of how long it had been since she finally gave up on her chores. The laundry she'd begun sorting was still in a heap on the bedroom floor, the mattress stripped and waiting for clean sheets, the vacuum in the middle of the living room floor.

A wineglass sat on the coffee table, its contents mostly untouched. Getting drunk to forget her problems had never been her style and she wasn't about to begin now.

Especially not because Chris had offered her a glimpse of something she didn't dare think about, not after years of schooling, studying and unwavering determination to achieve her goal. It would be too easy for her parents to continue ignoring Zoe if she stayed on in Hayseed Gulch, Montana, but when she became successful back in L.A. with the type of practice they understood and admired, they would have no choice but to acknowledge her achievement.

She would finally win their approval.

As she imagined her father introducing her to some of his hotshot friends at a fancy Hollywood premier, his chest puffed up with pride as he described her latest success, the cordless phone on the side table rang loudly. The sound startled her so badly that she nearly rolled off the couch.

The hospital always called her cell, as did most of her friends if they didn't feel like e-mailing. Putting aside the afghan and unfolding her legs, she approached the phone cautiously, as though it might explode, and peered at the caller ID. When she saw the name, she grabbed up the receiver, afraid the person at the other end might hang up without leaving a message.

"Mom?" Zoe asked. "Is everything all right?"

"Sure, Babe," Patrice replied. "I had a free minute before my ride arrives to pick me up, so I thought I'd check on my favorite daughter. How's it going out there in cowboy country?"

Zoe's throat tightened on a wave of sudden emotion. It took a moment for her to get a grip on herself so that she wouldn't sound weird. Knowing Patrice, she'd be too busy multi-tasking, going over her listings or checking her schedule on her PalmPilot to notice unless Zoe had a full-blown crying jag.

"Nothing much is happening here," Zoe said, clutching her wine. "How about you? Any big sales to report?"

Tired to the bone, Zoe pulled up in front of her apartment after work and dragged herself from her car. If she had thought the rumors had been embarrassing when she started seeing Chris, they didn't compare to the gossip since word got out about their breakup.

How was she supposed to concentrate on the practice of medicine while she was busy ignoring the fallout? The sympathetic comments and compassionate glances were bad enough. The smirks, winks and how-does-it-feel grins from a few of the male staff members whose passes she had rejected were worse. Even those incidents ranked lower on the discomfort level than seeing Chris at work.

She hadn't been called down to E.R. all morning, but her luck ran out at lunch where she had watched a female tech sidle up to Chris in the chow line like a snake that was about to swallow him whole. At least he hadn't appeared to be nursing a broken heart.

Later Zoe had nearly run him down when she came around a corner. They had both jumped back and made their excuses, but not before she'd seen the fatigue that lined his face and the lack of sparkle in his eyes.

Had she done that, she wondered again as she hurried through the rain to her apartment. Had she hurt him? It was the last thing she had intended.

"Zoe! Zoe, honey, wait up!"

She spun around, openmouthed with shock, in time to see her mother slam the door of a dark sedan, pop open a black umbrella and come rushing toward her.

It served her right for thinking this day couldn't get much worse, she thought dazedly. "What are you doing here?" she blurted, hardly caring how rude she must sound.

Patrice took her arm. "Let's not stand here in the rain," she said briskly. "I've come too darned far to get soaked in front of your door."

Meekly Zoe followed her, not at all surprised that her mother seemed to know exactly which way to go. She never went into a situation without doing her research first. Knowing Patrice, she had probably downloaded the floor plan of Zoe's building off the Internet.

Zoe's exhaustion seemed to triple, pressing her down like a giant boulder as they went silently up the steps. When she got to her entry, she fumbled with the key while her mother shook out her umbrella.

"You can leave that here," Zoe said as she opened the door.

"Won't someone steal it?" Patrice looked around warily, as though expecting a gang of umbrella thieves to leap from the shrubbery at any moment.

"No one will bother it," Zoe said. "This isn't L.A."

"Tell me about it. Do you have any idea how many flights I've been on?" With a last glance over her shoulder, Patrice followed Zoe inside.

The damned umbrella would probably blow away and Zoe would never hear the end of it. "I don't even know why you're here," she replied, her disgruntled tone reverberating in her own ears before a sudden thought drove the air from her lungs.

"Is something wrong with Dad?"

Her mother snorted as she unzipped her coat. "Do you have time to hear my list?" She reached out to pat Zoe's arm. "Divorcée humor, dear. As far as I know, your father is just peachy except for that paunch he's developed." She made a tsking sound. "And those unfortunate bags under his eyes. He really should see someone about those."

"Is something wrong with you?" Zoe asked, tension clutching at her like an eagle's talons.

"Can't I look in on you without there being some kind of family crisis?" her mother demanded, holding out her coat. "Would you hang this up somewhere?"

The notion that Zoe's mother would come all this way to look in on her was so foreign that Zoe was at a loss how to respond   diently she took off her jacket and hung them both in the closet.

"This looks like a decent place, but it could use a decorator," her mother murmured as she stood in the middle of the living room. "Could I have some tea after I use the little girls' room?"

"Of course." Zoe swallowed her impatience as she put the kettle on the stove. As usual, Patrice was the one running the show. "I'm sure you know where it is," Zoe added.

When her mother came back, Zoe pulled open the drawer where she kept the tea bags. "I have chamomile and red zinger."

Patrice sighed as she sat on the couch and crossed one leg clad in navy wool over the other. "Either one would be fine." Her tone made it clear that neither was acceptable so she would make do with whatever Zoe chose.

Silently Zoe fixed the tea. After she had set both cups

on the coffee table, she perched on the edge of a tweed armchair that faced the couch and tried to stifle her impatience.

"How was your trip?" she asked, trying to figure out what the hell she was supposed to do with her unexpected guest.

Despite her stylish hair and fresh makeup, Patrice looked tired. She shrugged, ignoring her tea. "First class isn't what it used to be, but the drive from Butte was okay."

"Why are you here?" Zoe blurted.

As though she could read her daughter's mind, Patrice sat back on the couch and folded her hands. "There was something in your voice when we talked on the phone." She glanced away, pressing her lips together as if to steady herself. Her apparent hesitation was totally out of character.

"You jumped on a plane because I sounded funny?" Zoe demanded.

Her mother's eyes blazed. "I was worried, okay? I know you're an adult and that you can take care of yourself, but I still have a mother's normal concerns."

The flow of words halted as though she had run out of steam. She looked down at her hands and then back at Zoe. "You're a bright, wonderful woman, but you try too hard to be perfect. Sometimes I'm afraid that maintaining the facade will burn you up."

Zoe had no idea what to say. Confused, she reached for her cup, but her hand shook, so she set it back down.

"I never knew that you could read me so well," she finally admitted. "It's a bit overwhelming."

Her mother's smile trembled as she patted the cushion next to her on the couch. "Come sit over here and tell me what's wrong."

With a sigh of defeat, Zoe did what she was told. Once she began to talk, she couldn't stop. By the time she was done, she had to excuse herself in order to get a box of tissues from the bathroom.

"Chris and I both knew I'd be leaving when my residency is done," Zoe concluded after she had blotted her eyes and blown her nose. "Our careers are taking us in two different directions."

Silence fell as she sipped the tea that was now barely warm.

"Don't make the same mistakes I did," her mother said after a moment.

"I thought you'd approve!" Zoe exclaimed. "I want to be successful so you and Daddy will be proud of me."

"Despite all our differences, your father and I have always been proud of you," her mother said firmly. "It's not our approval that matters anyway, it's what *you* want that's important."

"I'm doing what I want," Zoe said automatically.

Patrice patted her hand. "Then you can't go wrong." She glanced at the kitchen. "I'm hungry. Is there anywhere in this town to get a good meal?"

Zoe wasn't ready to revisit any of the places she'd gone with Chris, so they ended up eating at a small place near the motel where her mother had already checked in. Since her flight left Butte first thing in the morning and Zoe had to be at work, they said goodbye in the parking lot. It was dark, but the rain had stopped.

"Thank you so much for coming," Zoe said, fighting fresh tears. "It's great to see you. Are you sure you can't stay longer?"

"I've got a meeting," Patrice replied. "I'll leave a message on your cell in the morning." She stroked Zoe's arm. "Let me know when you've got time to come home for a visit and I'll send you an airline ticket."

Zoe hesitated, heart thumping hard. "Before you go, may I ask you something?"

Patrice's expression turned wary. "Of course. What is it?"

"Do you have any regrets?" Zoe blurted.

Her mother frowned. "About what?"

"About the choices you've made," Zoe persisted.

Patrice pressed her lips together. "I wish I had been more flexible, more willing to consider my options," she finally admitted. "There's more than one path to success, you know. Whichever one you choose, you'll be fine. I believe in you."

A car pulled into the parking lot and two couples got out, talking and laughing as they walked by.

"It's too late for Chris and me," Zoe said regretfully.

"Only if you let it be," her mother replied firmly, giving Zoe a hug. "Now go on home and get some rest. You've got an early shift in the morning."

"Thanks for everything," Zoe leaned over and kissed her mother's cheek. She was wearing a new scent, something light and tropical.

Before Zoe drove away, full of feelings and reactions to the visit, she tooted the car horn and Patrice waved.

After her mother's visit, Zoe was so busy at work that she hardly had time to think about their conversation. Each time she remembered her mother's comment about always being proud, she felt a warm glow in the region of her heart. Until now, Zoe had never realized how much pleasing her parents had influenced her choices. They hadn't been disappointed in her, just too caught in their own lives to pay much attention to their only child.

The knowledge that she no longer had to battle so hard for their approval was somehow freeing. It allowed her to think about what *she* wanted to do.

Nervously she knocked on the partly open door to Dr. Chester's office.

The director looked up, then beckoned Zoe to enter. "What's up?" Dr. Chester asked as she sat back and folded her hands behind her head. It seemed as though the older woman was always busy. Zoe wondered whether she ever got tired.

"Am I interrupting?" She hovered in the doorway.

"I've got a minute or two." Dr. Chester's gaze narrowed. "Something up? Would you like to close the door and sit down?"

Zoe did so, still not entirely sure why she was here. Once she was seated, she plucked at the hem of her skirt. "I've been thinking about our last talk," she said haltingly, "the one about the need for women's health-care in this area."

"I remember." The older woman's expression brightened. "Have you reconsidered the possibility of staying?"

"I'm not sure." Zoe squirmed restlessly, unused to having doubts about her decisions. "It partly depends on some…other issues."

"Ah-hah." Dr. Chester smiled. "If I'm not being too nosy, could one of those other issues have blond hair, a killer smile and a fondness for western boots?"

Zoe must have looked surprised, because her boss began to chuckle. "I may not put a lot of store in hospital gossip," she continued, "but I'm not oblivious to what's going on around me." Before Zoe could respond, she held up her hand. "Not that I would let some silly rumor influence my professional opinion of your performance in my department," she added. "Unless it affects your performance as a doctor, your personal life is your own business."

"Uh, thank you," Zoe replied, cheeks burning with embarrassment. "Do you think it would be a mistake to allow myself to be influenced by, um, elements outside work when it comes to making career choices?" she asked anxiously.

As soon as the question left her mouth, she wanted

to recall it. The woman seated behind the desk was her supervisor, not her guidance counselor.

"Good question," Dr. Chester replied before Zoe could apologize for asking it. "I have to tell you that I can't imagine being able to separate the two. That said, I must caution you that I also believe it's an absolute necessity to keep the personal and professional sides of your life in harmony so that one does not overshadow the other."

Zoe frowned. "How do you suggest I do that?"

Dr. Chester shook her head slowly. "Zoe, when I figure it out, I'll be sure to let you know. In the meantime this community is growing and we need doctors with your talent and empathy. You've got plenty of time to decide, so don't rush."

Zoe knew a dismissal when she heard one. "Thank you, Doctor," she replied. "I appreciate your support."

She went back to the nurses' station feeling more confused than ever. Having her goals mapped out, knowing exactly where she was headed, always made her feel more secure.

Suddenly something her mother had told her popped into her thoughts. *Whichever one you choose, you'll be fine. I believe in you.* Perhaps Zoe didn't need to have her entire future laid out in order to succeed. Maybe the way to proceed was by taking one step at a time.

The idea was a scary one.

The phone rang, making her jump as the receptionist seated behind the desk picked up the receiver. As she listened to the voice at the other end, she looked at Zoe. "I'll send Dr. Hart right down."

"That was Dr. Taylor in E.R.," she told Zoe after she'd hung up. "They need you down there stat. Possible miscarriage following a car accident."

Zoe's personal life had just been put on hold.

Forty-five minutes later, after the patient's contractions had been halted with medication, Zoe realized that she was done for the day. She was about to go back upstairs when the doors from the ambulance entrance opened to admit a paramedic pushing another gurney.

"Twenty-five-year-old female waitress, seven and a half months pregnant, fainted at work," he said, continuing on to recite the patient's vital signs as an intern and one of the nurses rushed over.

When the woman on the gurney turned her head, Zoe recognized her to be Juliet Rivera from The Hitching Post.

"Let me take her," Zoe told the intern. "Hi, Juliet. How are you feeling?"

"Still a little light-headed," Juliet replied softly. Her hands were pressed protectively to her rounded abdomen. "Is my baby going to be all right?"

"You're both going to be fine," Zoe reassured her as the gurney was taken to one of the cubicles. "Have you had any contractions?"

Juliet shook her head. "No, not at all. No cramping, either."

As the staff had her settled into a bed in one of the

curtained cubicles, one of the RNs on duty wrapped a blood pressure cuff around her arm. Another nurse poked her head through the curtain.

"She's been seeing Doc Codwell. Want me to call him?"

"Let him know that she's here and tell him what's happened," Zoe replied before donning her stethoscope and pressing it to Juliet's abdomen.

"I'm hearing a healthy fetal heartbeat," she told Juliet, whose eyes were huge with worry.

"I must work," Juliet babbled, "but I'll never forgive myself if it affects my baby."

"Let's not jump to conclusions just yet," Zoe cautioned.

"BP is one forty-five over ninety-two," the nurse said, "pulse is eighty-six."

"That's fine." Zoe patted Juliet's hand as she prayed softly in Spanish.

Carrie came back in and leaned down to Zoe's ear. "Dr. Codwell is with a patient at the clinic, but he'll come by as soon as he gets a chance."

"Is something wrong?" Juliet asked, shifting anxiously.

Zoe repeated what the nurse had told her. "Would it be all right for me to go ahead and finish examining you?" she asked.

Juliet nodded, lips trembling. "*Sí, sí.* I mean, yes, please."

Zoe ruled out previous dizzy spells, headaches and

heart palpitations. "And no recent spotting or contractions?"

Juliet shook her head. "I just felt dizzy and then, bam. The next thing I knew, I was on the floor."

After Zoe had finished, she took Juliet's hand in hers. The poor woman's dark eyes were glistening with tears.

"Everything looks fine," Zoe told her. "The important thing is that you aren't in labor and the baby's heartbeat is strong. Now I'm going to order a blood test to make sure you aren't anemic."

"What can I do to take better care?" Juliet asked.

Zoe sighed. Obviously Juliet's choices were limited. "Eat regular meals and get off your feet as often as possible." She stood up. "You need to take a little time off, at least a couple of days, and rest up."

Juliet nodded tearfully. "I will."

Zoe's heart ached for her situation. Chris had confided that Juliet had been through some very tough times. Her brother had been killed and the baby's father abandoned her, so she had no one to watch out for her.

"Do you need a note for work?" Zoe asked.

"Martha has been good to me. She will understand."

Zoe patted her hand. "Take care of yourself and have a healthy baby."

Once again Carrie appeared through the striped curtain. "Dr. Codwell is on his way."

"As soon as I talk to him, I'll send him right in,"

Zoe promised Juliet, who thanked her profusely before she left.

As Zoe walked tiredly back up the stairs a little while later without seeing Chris, she couldn't help but wonder what patients like Juliet Rivera would do if there weren't enough doctors and clinics in Thunder Canyon to treat them.

Chapter Thirteen

As Zoe climbed the hospital staircase, ahead of her was a nurse she knew slightly. Frances wore her gray hair in a tight perm and her white nylon uniform clung to her wide rear end. The entire staff knew that she was one of the biggest gossips at TCG.

Zoe's heart skittered in her chest when Chris appeared at the top of the stairs. After the way she had acted, what chance did she have to make things right?

When he drew closer, he winked at Frances and nodded to Zoe. Although his smile didn't dim, she could tell that his expression was guarded.

"Sorry that I missed you in the E.R.," he said as he passed her.

Briefly she told him about Juliet. When Zoe reached the top of the stairs, Frances was still hovering there.

"That man should be on the cover of *Vanity Fair*," she exclaimed, hand fluttering over her ample bosom. Her small eyes brimmed with curiosity as she studied Zoe.

"What went wrong between the two of you?" Frances probed, lowering her voice. "He's got to be the best catch in this county—and probably in the entire state—if you ask me."

For a moment, Zoe was taken aback by the other woman's nosiness, but then she had an idea. Glancing around, she grabbed Frances's arm, practically dragging her to the side of the corridor. "Promise you won't tell anyone?" Zoe asked softly.

Frances's eyes bugged out. She nodded so enthusiastically that—for a moment—Zoe feared her head might fall off her shoulders and roll across the floor. "Of course," she breathed. "You can tell me anything, cross my heart!"

Zoe leaned even closer. "It was my fault," she whispered conspiratorially. "I made a stupid mistake and let him get away."

"Do you love him?" the nurse asked.

For once Zoe didn't bother to keep her emotions hidden. "He's the one for me," she admitted. "I love him with all my heart."

Frances patted her arm. "It's never too late to make things right."

"I wouldn't know where to start." Zoe shook her head sadly. "I probably shouldn't have said anything. Be sure to keep it between you and me."

Frances's eyes were already darting back and forth as people passed them in the corridor. "Of course, dear," she told Zoe. "I won't breathe a word to anyone."

As they parted company, she hurried away so fast that Zoe was surprised the thick soles of her orthopedic shoes didn't burn rubber.

For several days, Zoe endured the curious glances and the whispers that died abruptly whenever she appeared.

"Has he said anything?" Vadivu asked when they met in the cafeteria on a break. She had confided to Zoe that her romance with John seemed to be going well.

There was no point in pretending ignorance. "Not a word."

"Maybe he doesn't know," Vadivu suggested hopefully after she had taken a drink of her juice.

"Thanks to Frances, the entire hospital knows," Zoe retorted. "I just have to face the fact that my feelings no longer matter. It's my own fault."

The other resident drained her glass and scooted back her chair. "I told John I'd come by the lab." She gave Zoe's shoulders a quick hug. "I'm sorry."

After Vadivu left, Zoe finished her soda, refusing to let the curious glances drive her from the cafeteria. At the next table, Dr. Codwell—smelling of cigars, as usual—was talking to a colleague in a booming voice.

"I don't know about you," he grumbled, "but my practice is getting too busy. It's affecting my golf game."

"I've had to hire another nurse and I'm thinking about taking on an associate," the other doctor replied, his tone disgruntled. "If the rumors are true and the deed to the mine is missing, this town will be crawling with speculators, developers and God knows who else before we know it."

None of it mattered to Zoe. If she had lost Chris for good, every minute of her remaining months would be agony.

Without bothering to finish her soda or her break, she left the cafeteria. When she got back to the maternity wing, the receptionist called out to her.

"Dr. Hart, I just got a message that you're needed in the E.R. There's been some kind of altercation out at the mine and several people were injured. Dr. Taylor wants you down there stat."

At least he was still willing to work with her, Zoe thought grimly as she headed down the stairs. She may have screwed up her personal life, but her career appeared to be on track.

An hour later, the board was cleared of patients and the E.R. waiting room was miraculously empty as the staff gathered around the triage desk. Chris had disappeared.

"This place won't be the same if Dr. Taylor should

leave," one of the nurses muttered as she moved a stack of charts. "What would we do without him?"

Zoe froze. "Leave?" she echoed, unconcerned that her interest would no doubt make her appear even more pathetic than before. "When?"

"I don't know," the nurse replied. "All I heard was that he's been looking into positions out of state."

Oh, God. Was it possible that the gossip she had started so impulsively was driving him away? Maybe he was attempting to spare her because he no longer loved her. Her mind whirled with confusion.

It was exactly the kind of thing he might do—sacrifice his own contentment in order to spare her from the embarrassment of being around a man who didn't return her feelings. What had she done?

She leaned over the counter as heartbreak and regret threatened to overwhelm her. She had to get out of the E.R. before she started crying or her humiliation would be complete. And then when she had regained control of her emotions, she would have to convince him not to leave the home that he loved.

"I heard that he might go to California," someone else said.

California? That couldn't be right. Surely he would have said something.

"Oh, would you look at those flowers," Carrie exclaimed before Zoe could escape.

Chris was carrying a large bouquet of red roses as

he came over to the counter where Zoe stood. His usual smile was absent, his expression somber.

She was dying to ask about his plans, but her questions would have to wait for a more opportune time. As she moved out of his way, she noticed that the flowers weren't in a vase.

"Where are you going?" he asked, shifting so that he blocked her escape.

"I thought you wanted to set them on the counter." She ached to reach out and touch him. The scent of the roses filled her nostrils, making her head spin. *I can't do this,* she thought. *Not here.*

Moving closer yet, he held out the bouquet. "These are for you," he said softly.

For once the E.R. was quiet and no one said a word as she accepted them.

"They're beautiful," she murmured, tucking them in the crook of her arm as she struggled to read his expression. Hope flared at what she saw in his face and her legs began to tremble. "I don't understand."

"I just heard the rumor that's been going around," he said. "Apparently no one had the nerve to tell me about it until I ran into Willie this morning."

"Oh?" she squeaked past the sudden lump in her throat as she noticed the maintenance man leaning on his broom, watching avidly.

Chris patted his pocket. "These are some e-mails

I've written to hospitals in L.A.," he said. "I've been researching the job market in that area."

Someone groaned and was promptly shushed.

Zoe's entire body began to shake. The roses trembled in her arms, so she set them aside.

"Why?" she whispered, hardly able to breathe as she stared into the face of the man who had become her entire world.

"There's a rumor going around that you love me." A collective sigh seemed to go up from the people around them as he dropped to one knee. "For once, I hope with everything that's in me, that the grapevine got it right." His gaze was locked on hers like a laser, making her forget everyone but him.

"It's true." she exclaimed. "I do love you with all my heart."

The tension seemed to drain from his face. "Thank God," he whispered hoarsely. "Marry me, Zoe. I swear, I'll follow you anywhere."

"She already said 'I do,'" someone murmured.

Tears of joy threatened to blur Zoe's eyes. "You don't have to leave here," she protested, realizing it was true. "I've fallen for Thunder Canyon. If you really want me, I'll marry you both."

As applause burst out around them, Chris stood up and pulled her into his arms for a tender kiss. For a long moment, they held each other close before he finally let her go.

"Let's find somewhere private and make some plans," he suggested.

Zoe reached up and laid her hand against his cheek. "That's one prescription I'm happy to take."

* * * * *

Coming in April 2005
The next book in
MONTANA MAVERICKS:
GOLD RUSH GROOMS
THEIR UNEXPECTED FAMILY
By reader favorite
Judy Duarte
When pregnant waitress Juliet Rivera is ordered to stay off her feet, a handsome out-of-town reporter rushes to her aid. But can this cynical stranger find love with the beautiful mom-to-be?
Available wherever Silhouette Books are sold.

Silhouette®

SPECIAL EDITION™

Don't miss the exciting conclusion of
The Fortunes of Texas: Reunion
three-book continuity
in Silhouette Special Edition

IN A TEXAS MINUTE
by Stella Bagwell

Available April 2005
Silhouette Special Edition #1677

When Sierra Mendoza was left with an abandoned
baby, she turned to her closest friend and confidant,
Alex Calloway. While taking care of the infant,
Sierra and Alex's relationship went from platonic
to passionate. But would deep-seated scars from Alex's
past prevent them from becoming a ready-made family?

THE
FORTUNES
OF TEXAS™
Reunion

The price of privilege. The power of family.

Available at your favorite retail outlet.

Silhouette®

Where love comes alive™

SPECIAL EDITION™

presents the first book in a compelling
new miniseries by reader favorite

Christine Flynn

**This quiet Vermont town inspires old lovers
to reunite—and new loves to blossom!**

TRADING SECRETS
SE #1678, available April 2005

Free-spirited, ambitious Jenny Baker thought she'd
left Maple Mountain behind forever. But her city
life didn't go quite as well as she'd planned, and
now Jenny is back home, trying to put her life back
together—and trying to keep the truth about her
return under wraps. Until she's hired by handsome
local doctor Greg Reid, who ignites feelings she'd
thought she'd put to rest long ago. And when
Greg uncovers Jenny's deepest secret, he makes
her an offer she can't refuse....

Where love comes alive™

If you enjoyed what you just read,
then we've got an offer you can't resist!

Take 2 bestselling love stories FREE!

Plus get a FREE surprise gift!

Clip this page and mail it to Silhouette Reader Service™

IN U.S.A.	IN CANADA
3010 Walden Ave.	P.O. Box 609
P.O. Box 1867	Fort Erie, Ontario
Buffalo, N.Y. 14240-1867	L2A 5X3

YES! Please send me 2 free Silhouette Special Edition® novels and my free surprise gift. After receiving them, if I don't wish to receive anymore, I can return the shipping statement marked cancel. If I don't cancel, I will receive 6 brand-new novels every month, before they're available in stores! In the U.S.A., bill me at the bargain price of $4.24 plus 25¢ shipping and handling per book and applicable sales tax, if any*. In Canada, bill me at the bargain price of $4.99 plus 25¢ shipping and handling per book and applicable taxes**. That's the complete price and a savings of at least 10% off the cover prices—what a great deal! I understand that accepting the 2 free books and gift places me under no obligation ever to buy any books. I can always return a shipment and cancel at any time. Even if I never buy another book from Silhouette, the 2 free books and gift are mine to keep forever.

235 SDN DZ9D
335 SDN DZ9E

Name	(PLEASE PRINT)	
Address	Apt.#	
City	State/Prov.	Zip/Postal Code

Not valid to current Silhouette Special Edition® subscribers.

Want to try two free books from another series?
Call 1-800-873-8635 or visit www.morefreebooks.com.

* Terms and prices subject to change without notice. Sales tax applicable in N.Y.
** Canadian residents will be charged applicable provincial taxes and GST.
   All orders subject to approval. Offer limited to one per household.
   ® are registered trademarks owned and used by the trademark owner and or its licensee.

SPED04R   ©2004 Harlequin Enterprises Limited

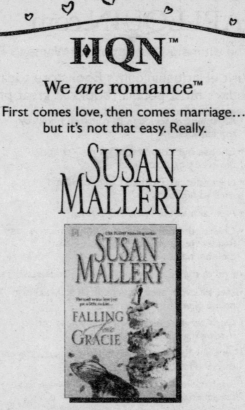